IF THESE PRISON WALLS COULD TALK

WHAT WOULD THEY SAY...

DR. KEVIN E. DOLPHIN

Lime Press

If These Prison Walls Could Talk What Would They Say
by Dr. Kevin E. Dolphin

ISBN: 978-1-953584-63-2 (Paperback)
ISBN: 978-1-953584-62-5 (Hardback)
ISBN: 978-1-953584-64-9 (E-book)

Printed in the United States of America

Lime Press LLC
425 West Washington Street
Suffolk VA, 23434 Suite 4
https://www.lime-press.com/

"Dr. Dolphin has put together a powerful book from his painful experiences to give us a realistic outlook on the broken prison system. As a legislator, it has given me insight on the changes we have to make for a fairer system that heals people instead of breaking them."

Pennsylvania State Representative Patty Kim

It is with pleasure that I am responding to the request to review Dr. Dolphin's manuscript, **"If Prison Walls Could Talk."** The pleasure comes from a mutual commitment, Dr. Dolphin's and mine, to promoting/providing inmates with "self-help/self-definition" programs. I am also impressed by how he has chosen to redirect his life and to engage others to change and improve theirs.

Reflecting on the manuscript, I note three interwoven components with research on a very punitive corrections system and statistics on the composition of the inmates setting the stage. The second component, in narrative form, focuses on factors such as poverty, race, education, social status and family composition with encouragement to face and address the issues. The third component, and to me a very significant one, is the "Walls" talk. As an example, I am attaching a talk that succinctly and effectively conveys the message. The manuscript also contains copies of letters, lectures, charts to support the author's mission.

As to readership, this is information that should have the widest audience: policy makers, activists, inmates, the general public. It should also be part of schools' curricula because it exposes realities with the potential for destruction of lives. There is also a program model for preparing inmates with skills for community reentry.

Sincerely,

Irene C. Baird, D.Ed.
Affliate Assistant Professor
Penn State Harrisburg

Pastor Nathaniel Kendrick,

Itinerant Elder AME Church, 7th Episcopal District, MDive.

Writes…………

The collateral damages of imprisonment are enormous, and the lack of intentional rehabilitation contribute to the unaddressed issues behind prison walls. Dr. Kevin Dolphin writes an impactful, thoughtful and meaningful illustration of the actual experiences behind prison walls. His depiction portrays the physical, mental and emotional challenges overlooked by the prison system. Spiritual experiences and ideas develop the guide for this author's inspiration of the words in this book. I recommend this book as a tool for those who desire to serve others. A testimony of truth for family, community, preachers and faith leaders to understand the journey of those who have relied on the walls to speak. A simple and plain read that reveals truth and revelation.

After spending nearly two decades in and out of prison, I finally realized that there had to be a better way.

With the help of Dr. Dolphin, I was able to break the chains of mental and physical prison. I attended the programs he offered behind the wall, as well as walked with him for several years, during our incarceration.

This book is a must read for EVERYONE!

The insight he gives is right on point. Anyone who is seeking understanding and change, look no further.

IF THESE PRISON WALLS COULD TALK Vol. 1

Is what inmates, family members, community members, the judicial system and legislators need as a guide.

Mr. Emett Eden

IF THESE PRISON WALLS COULD TALK

WHAT WOULD THEY SAY...

DR. KEVIN E. DOLPHIN

Lime Press

If These Prison Walls Could Talk What Would They Say
by Dr. Kevin E. Dolphin

This book is written to provide information and motivation to readers. Its purpose isn't to render any type of psychological, legal, or professional advice of any kind. The content is the sole opinion and expression of the author, and not necessarily that of the publisher.

Copyright © 2020 by Dr. Kevin E. Dolphin

ISBN: 978-1-953584-63-2 (Paperback)
ISBN: 978-1-953584-62-5 (Hardback)
ISBN: 978-1-953584-64-9 (E-book)

Printed in the United States of America

Lime Press LLC
425 West Washington Street
Suffolk VA, 23434 Suite 4
https://www.lime-press.com/

"Dr. Dolphin has put together a powerful book from his painful experiences to give us a realistic outlook on the broken prison system. As a legislator, it has given me insight on the changes we have to make for a fairer system that heals people instead of breaking them."

Pennsylvania State Representative Patty Kim

It is with pleasure that I am responding to the request to review Dr. Dolphin's manuscript, **"If Prison Walls Could Talk."** The pleasure comes from a mutual commitment, Dr. Dolphin's and mine, to promoting/providing inmates with "self-help/self-definition" programs. I am also impressed by how he has chosen to redirect his life and to engage others to change and improve theirs.

Reflecting on the manuscript, I note three interwoven components with research on a very punitive corrections system and statistics on the composition of the inmates setting the stage. The second component, in narrative form, focuses on factors such as poverty, race, education, social status and family composition with encouragement to face and address the issues. The third component, and to me a very significant one, is the "Walls" talk. As an example, I am attaching a talk that succinctly and effectively conveys the message. The manuscript also contains copies of letters, lectures, charts to support the author's mission.

As to readership, this is information that should have the widest audience: policy makers, activists, inmates, the general public. It should also be part of schools' curricula because it exposes realities with the potential for destruction of lives. There is also a program model for preparing inmates with skills for community reentry.

Sincerely,

Irene C. Baird, D.Ed.
Affliate Assistant Professor
Penn State Harrisburg

Pastor Nathaniel Kendrick,

Itinerant Elder AME Church, 7th Episcopal District, MDive.

Writes…………

The collateral damages of imprisonment are enormous, and the lack of intentional rehabilitation contribute to the unaddressed issues behind prison walls. Dr. Kevin Dolphin writes an impactful, thoughtful and meaningful illustration of the actual experiences behind prison walls. His depiction portrays the physical, mental and emotional challenges overlooked by the prison system. Spiritual experiences and ideas develop the guide for this author's inspiration of the words in this book. I recommend this book as a tool for those who desire to serve others. A testimony of truth for family, community, preachers and faith leaders to understand the journey of those who have relied on the walls to speak. A simple and plain read that reveals truth and revelation.

After spending nearly two decades in and out of prison, I finally realized that there had to be a better way.

With the help of Dr. Dolphin, I was able to break the chains of mental and physical prison. I attended the programs he offered behind the wall, as well as walked with him for several years, during our incarceration.

This book is a must read for EVERYONE!

The insight he gives is right on point. Anyone who is seeking understanding and change, look no further.

IF THESE PRISON WALLS COULD TALK Vol. 1

Is what inmates, family members, community members, the judicial system and legislators need as a guide.

Mr. Emett Eden

Prologue

If These Prison Walls Could Talk, would they praise the courts for all of the criminals that are confined behind bars? Would they demand harsher penalties and stiffer laws? Or would they beg for relief due to all of the over crowdedness?...

If These Prison Walls Could Talk, would they speak of all of the injustice that has been handed down by the judicial system over the past four hundred years and some change?...

If These Prison Walls Could Talk, would they tell the tragic story of my mothers' final seconds on this place we call earth?...

If These Prison Walls Could Talk, would they yell at the top of their lungs or whisper about the many men/women who have been separated from their children?...

If These Prison Walls Could Talk, what would they say? Would they preach the need for change? Would they hand down the wisdom that they have acquired? Would they direct the youth or would they turn their backs, keep their mouths shut and condemn the fallen ones like so many others have?...

If These Prison Walls Could Talk, what would they actually say?...

Dr. Kevin. E. Dolphin

Dedications

To Dorothy M. Radcliff.

If These Prison Walls Could Talk, they would tell the story of the angel who earned her wings.

- Still I Rise…

Born into a world filled with falsities and illusions,

where disfunction is recognized as functional…

Still I Rise…

Given hardships and inequality to supplement for

A father who was mysteriously murdered in the streets…

Still I Rise…

Misguided as a youth, separated from my mother by

Prison bars at the tender age of 14…

Still I Rise…

Momentarily lost to the judicial system, where I spent nearly half my life trying to break the mental, spiritual, physical and emotional chainz of imprisonment…

Still I Rise…

Traumatized as a young boy, finding my true identity as a man, searching for redemption in a society where ones own reflection in the mirror creates more corruption and lies…

Still I Rise…

By GOD's grace and mercy…

Still I Rise…

The incomparable Dr. Kevin E. Dolphin

Table of Contents

Forward

After being sentenced to fifteen years in federal prison for drug trafficking, life as I once knew it existed no more... The false reality that I had been living in for so long had suddenly evaporated – Forcing me to finally take account of my actions and emerge from the matrix of mental poverty that I had been stuck in for nearly thirty years. Uncertain of my future, I began applying myself in an endeavor to uncover the answer as to why so many people end up on the pathway to prison; just as I had... Once trapped inside of that revolving door, the cycle of recidivism begins and the chances of breaking the chainz of enslavement become almost impossible... **"In order to find the cause, one must get to the root of the problem."** – It was once said that, once you begin to know yourself, you begin to know all things around you!

While studying my surroundings for over a decade, I began to piece together this analogy. As astounding as it may be at times, the truth cannot be ignored... Walk with me down the long, lonely, dark, cold corridors of some of the places that have engulfed the souls of countless men and women. As we enter through the front gates, keep in mind that **IF THESE PRISON WALLS COULD TALK**, the stories that they would tell would leave the masses looking at the judicial system in a total different light...

Dr. Kevin E. Dolphin

Chapter One
"The Game"

As we enter the front gates of the United States of America's penal system, take a walk with me down the long, cold, dark, damp corridor that leads to cell Block-A; **"The Game"**…

Making positive changes in our prison system is one that is very challenging and needs all of our help. Most of the methods used by the judicial system are ineffective. For the many tax payers who continue to foot the bill, I am quite sure that you will agree that it doesn't take a genius to see that.

In a swollen prison population, the government has created massive over crowdedness, with petty criminals, drug addicts, who should be enrolled in treatment programs and illegal immigrants, who have been given lengthy sentences that usually doesn't match their crime.

Along with the inflated bubble that seems as if it is ready to burst at any given moment, some of the conditions on the inside are horrendous. I am not one to say that prison should be a resort or vacation for those that may have broken the law, but being a man who now views the "system" through an unbiased and fair eye, I can honestly say that what many inmates are going through on the inside can be considered a living hell…. Health treatment is poorer than some third world countries, there are not enough jobs, and in most institutions, the rations of food are so small that it forces many of the men/women, who have no outside support or employment to resort to stealing… That creates another problem, which I will address in a later chapter.

With the absence of a lot of programs from lack of funding, few or no trades are available and countless industrial factories resorting to pay wages that could be considered by most, modern day slavery; many of the inmates who often times find themselves locked away in prison for lengthy periods of time are released with little or no money, no training skills to help them compete in a tight job market, and in a large number of cases, no place to live. Their criminal identity is what most of them cling to as a means of being able to survive.

In my opinion, while doing time, inmates should be shown various ways to communicate, how to solve problems, given treatment for their illnesses (mental way of thinking), and extensive job training to help them become productive citizens once they are released back into society. They should be equipped with skills that will make their experiences in the outside world something that they can adapt to and take control of. Their release should be something that they look forward to, instead of something to feel apprehensive about. They must be given the tools that will help change and shape their behavior. –Without the change of ones thoughts and behaviors, the individual will always resort back to what lead him/her to prison.

Despite being one who has found myself on the opposite side of the law for most of my life, I am in full agreement and am very much aware that all inmates aren't ready or feel that they need to change; but I also feel that the ones who are ready and put for the effort, should be fully supported.

As I took a look around many of the institutions that I once inhabited, I realized that there were no "real" prison groups; such as mens discussion groups that give inmates an outlet that allows them to come together, talk about various issues and come up with solutions to many of the problems that they face while doing time.

Feeling the need for such a program, I sat down with one of my counselors at FCI Ray Brook and designed "Back To The Future"… It is a twelve week discussion group, that gives each individual a chance to reflect and take an in depth look at their past, assist them in coping with their present situation, and provides them with an opportunity to chart a successful course to their future.

Discussions include:

- Family Relations
- Past Mistakes
- Future Goals, short/long term
- How to do time productively
- Education
- Communication skills

Inmates must feel valued if their worth is ever to exceed what they have felt in the past. They should feel a sense of love, connection and acceptance.

If given the proper chance, a great number of men/women who are in prison can return back to society and become great leaders. Their experiences, tragedies, failures and successes can be used to provide someone else with a compelling story that might save their lives or perhaps prevent them from travelling down a long prison corridor that leads to nowhere.

That brings me to: **"The Game"**…

Imagine yourself walking into a casino, where all of the crap tables, card tables, slot machines and roulette tables were set up and rigged for the house to win. Would you play?... I certainly hope not!…

For those of us who may find ourselves participating in the act of committing crime, on any level, we foolishly and most times unknowingly become victims of "The Game"; which I intend to focus on at this point…

Allow me to venture deeper into this subject- let us take a look at the so called "Drug Game." For decades, it has only benefited those who created it and served its intended purpose. For the man or woman who had been farced into thinking that by selling drugs they were creating a better life for themselves and their families-they were sadly mistaken. Although it may appear from the outside that life is being lived on a grand scale, inner turmoil and disfunctions within the unit are highly probable. How can one profess to build up his or her inner structure, when they are tearing down everything around them? That is exactly what occurs when an individual takes part in the drug trade. Take a moment and evaluate each of your communities. Are they crime ridden, drug infested and most times unsafe for anyone besides untamed savages to inhabit? Because of the dealers who often create an unsafe environment for all of those around them, children end up with no place to play, the people who once sat out on their porches to enjoy the nice weather are forced into their homes and older folks are scared to take a walk to the corner store.

For those of you who may lack the understanding, this is how the "Drug Game" usually plays itself out: The dealer sells drugs, accumulates money, cars, homes and other assets, destroys community in the process, often corrupts the morals of the youth, gets arrested, goes to prison, loses cars, homes and assets and becomes a burden on their family…

Just as there are two sides to a coin, know that there are two side to "The Game." Heads, they win; tails, you lose.

Heads:	Glitz	Jewelry
	Glamour	Houses
	Cars	Fast women
Tails:	Prison	Broken Homes
	Hardship	Unsafe communities
	Death	

The illusions that are given off by the so called "Game" attract and trap those who are unaware of both sides. Things that often seem pleasing to the eye are most times detrimental to ones own very existence. At the end of the road all of the glitz, glamour, cars, houses and fast women, the shocking realization of prison, hardship, death, broken homes and unsafe communities await.

For generations upon generations, men and women have partook in a game which neither of them were ever fully aware of the underline rules. In order to play a game and be successful at it, you must fully understand the rules. Do you agree?.. But what about when there are no rules or when those who make the rules change them whenever they feel as if the "players" are getting ahead. How can you win?... You can't … Try and try as you may, but you will never be able to outsmart the fox. – The definition of insanity is continuing to do the same thing over and over again, expecting to receive a different result.

: An allowance of control over your thinking dictates your actions. When a man/woman is trained to think a certain way, there is never a need to worry about them acting contrary to what has been implanted into their minds. Instilled with unfavorable qualities and inferiorities, they will feel out of place when presented with a picture of moral clarity and self-esteem. Continuing the cycle that has been adopted by their forefathers, he/she remains engulfed in a world filled with back doors and illogical ideology.

How does a family who has been plagued with such a destructive disorder escape the grips of mental impoverishment that has crippled an entire body of people? Continue to walk with me a little further down the corridor as we examine the efforts of what takes place when families who have become dysfunctional blindly allow "The Game" to dictate the course of their lives. Somewhere along the way, we will find a solution to this catastrophic problem…

What happens to the structure of a family when the man is removed as the head or the women is vanquished from her duties? It automatically becomes weak! Why? Anytime that either parent is removed from the home, roles automatically switch, and responsibilities shift. In the case of the father going to prison, the mother has to step outside of her natural position and play his part, the son, who often times is nothing but a child begins to think of himself as the man of the house, despite his lack of understanding of what a real man is and the daughter is left without a figure to show her how she should be treated and respected by her male counterpart. Therefore, leaving her searching for the true definition of love and affection.

Now, in the case of the woman being absent, the father has to take on the role of the nurturer, the son is left without motherly affection and adoration and the daughter begins her life long struggle to identify with all of the traits that a real women should have. In either case, the family is dysfunctional and everyone involved in the equation is deprived of something that they should be getting. This is where the cycle begins.

If the root of the weed is not destroyed, it continues to grow and cause destruction throughout the garden. Therefore, we must exterminate it. Preventing the chances of it **from spreading like a deadly germ. How can we do this? Let us begin with the parents.** As we look at the psychological makeup of a child, understand that the off-spring has gathered genetic traits from its mother and father. Then there are the things that he or she is taught while growing up; consciously or unconsciously. How many times have our parents or we as parents told our children to do one thing, then they witness us doing another? In all actuality, this send mixed messages. Having studied how the human mind works for the past decade and a half, I am aware that physical images and actions override verbal messages. That is one of the reasons why television and social media has such as strong influence when it comes to our social system. Without the proper guidance, certain programs, movies and videos become our childrens main teachers. Also, be aware that a mother or father can only teach a child what they know. If the parents are misinformed, then what type of information do you think that they will pass on to those that come after them? That is one of the reasons why it is so important for one to be educated in ethics, moral standings, financial literacy, truama and the profound effect that religion has on our views. Knowledge is power. Therefore, we must gather the tools that we need in order for us to rise above the mind state of ignorance that so many of us live in. Until that is done, the cycle of genocide will continue, the doors of recidivism will remain open and the potential leaders of tomorrow will continue to allow their true identities to allude them. Instead of becoming a State Senator, they wind up becoming a number in a state or federal penitentiary.

Fingerprints

After being fingerprinted, my life was never the same…I was given
a number, classified, and beat down in shame…

No longer am I looked at as an upstanding citizen; guilty until
proven innocent…Traces of black ink still soil my hand…

No longer a name, I'm identified by a number…Echoes of cell
doors slamming at night are reminiscent of thunder…

Although I've only spent one night in jail, I was booked,
fingerprinted and cast into a living hell…

Author: Dr. Kevin E. Dolphin

A Nation Incarcerated

According to a study done by Charles Lemo, in 2010;

- The United States has the highest documented incarceration rate in the world, with a nearly one percent of its population behind bars. One in ninety-nine adults are incarcerated. No society ever recorded in history has imprisoned more of its citizens than the U.S...

- There are more black 17 year olds in prison than in college...

- As a percentage of the population, we imprison more than twice as much as South Africa. Our rate of incarceration is more than three times higher than Irans and more than six times higher than Chinas...

- Stephen Fry notes; prisons are a big business. He goes as far as suggesting that we have reinvented the slave trade.

- Perhaps that's a bit much, but certain things are hard to ignore. While it is illegal to import manufactured goods made by forced prison labor, it's not illegal to produce them domestically. Take the Federal Prison Industries (FPI) for example; a self-sustaining, self-funded corporation, established in 1934 by executive order; who also employs more than 30,000 inmates in over 100 FPI factories in prisons across the U.S. Despite downturns in certain sectors, because of the recession, UNICOR's "employees" have grown by a third in the last decade. FPI, who manufactures under the trade name UNICOR, manufactures products such as office furniture, clothing, beds and linens, electronics equipment and eye wear. Including manufacturing certain items for the United States military, it also offers services including data entry, bulk mailing, laundry services, recycling, and refurbishing of vehicle components. Twenty one percent of U.S. manufactured office furniture is produced by prison labor...

- Minimum estimate of annual value of prison and jail industrial out-put exceeded $2billion dollars in 2006, with FPI accounting for over a quarter of that amount. In 2009,

FPI reported sales of $885 million. The minimum wage paid at UNICOR plant is $0.23 an hours. By of comparison, the minimum wage paid in Haiti is $0.30 an hour, while the average hourly earnings of a non-prisoner U.S. worker making office furniture is $13.04...

- Nevada pays its prison work force $0.13 an hour. Georgia and Texas do not pay a wage at all.

- Here are some other disturbing facts:

- The United States has just over four percent of the worlds population, but over twenty five percent of the worlds prison population...

- The Peoples Republic Of China ranks second with 1.5 million inmates, while having four times the population, thus having only about 18% of the U.S. incarceration rate.

- On a per capita basis, the United States has the highest prison population rate in the world, with 756 per 100,000 of the national population behind bars. We are followed by Russia (629), Rwanda (604) St. Kitts & Nevis (588), Cub (.531), U.S. Virgin Is. (512), British Virgin Is. (488), Palau (478), Belarus (465), Belize (488), Bahamas (422), Georgia (425), American Samoa (410), Grenada (408) and Anguilla (401).

- According to the U.S. Bureau of Justice Statistics (BJS): "In 2008, over 7.3 million people were on probation, in jail or prison, or on parole at year end – 3.2% of all U.S. adult residents or 1 in every 31 adults...

- The country's prison population topped 2 million inmates for the first time in history on June 30, 2008. Meaning that the U.S. prison population has grown nearly 50% in just eight years. At year end of 2008, the total incarcerated population equaled 2,424,279 inmates...

- Seventy percent of prisoners in the United States are non-whites, even though non-whites make up only a third of the U.S. population. One out of every twenty black males over the age of 18 are in prison. That compares to one in 180 white males over the age of 18. In five states, between one in 13 and one in 14 black men are in prison. One in nine African American males will spend at least one year in jail over the course of their lifetimes...

- Most drug offenders are white- five times as many whites use drugs as blacks, yet blacks comprise the great majority of drug offenders sent to prison. Of the 253,3000 state prison inmates serving time for drug offenses at year end 2005, 113,5000 (44.8%) were black, 51,100 (20.2%) were Hispanic, and 72,300 (28.5%) were white.

- The non-violent prison population alone is larger than the combined populations of Wyoming and Alaska…

- According to the American Corrections Association, the average daily cost per state prison inmate per day in the U.S. is $67.55. State prisons held 253,300 inmates for drug offenses in 2005. That means states spent approximately $17,110,415 per day to imprison drug offenders, or $6,245,301,475 per year…

- State spent $42.89 billion on prison and corrections in 2005 alone. To compare, states only spent $24.69 billion on public assistance. From 1989 to 1996, California built 21 new prisons and only one new university.

- Between 1979 and 2000, the number of additional prisons ranged from 19 prisons in Missouri to 120 prisons in Texas. The growth in Texas equates to an extraordinary average annual increase of 5.7 additional prisons per year over the 21 year period. Over this time frame, Texas increased its prisons by a stunning 706 percent…

Black and White

"This book is not about black or white, but it has everything to do with black and white."

Although I am an African American male in America, who has been faced with a lot of unfair obstacles, that often seem to have been put in place to cause me to fail, I blame no one but myself for my situation….

Did you know that black men are 6.5% times more likely to be in prison than white men?..

- Do your history; the relationship between race and crime has been a specific area of study for criminologist, which date back to the late 19th century. Social and economic conditions are central factors that contribute to criminal behavior. Regardless of race, creed or color. Despite those behaviors, whites seem to receive lesser penalties than those who are black and Hispanic. As of the writing of this book, almost 10.4% of the entire African American male population in the U.S. aged 25 to 29 is incarcerated in some type of county, state or federal correctional facility; which is in comparison to 1.2% white males and 2.4% hispanics. The number of black men who are in prison tripled in the last couple of decades. It has been noted that more African American men are in jail than in college.

The relationships between race and crime in the United States has been a controversial topic for more than a century. Issues has centered around cause and effect factors; disproportional representation of minority groups; and bias judgement throughout the judicial system. Arrests, prosecutions and incarcerations are also main factors that must be looked at when proper analysis are made. Environment, social status and other external, as well as, internal factors lead to criminal behavior.

Throughout history, crime rate and statistics have taken center stage in the discussion of the relationship between race, environment and social status in the U.S. Criminologist, as well as, sociologist have used crime rate statistics and environment as principal guides in their findings. Many do not take into account how most minority groups are misrepresented in many of these cases…

I once read about a case where two different individuals, one black and one white committed the same crime, but due to the differences in their race, environments and social economic standings, the black male received a much harsher penalty than did his white counterpart. As I studied this case, I took all of these factors into account, while doing my best to make an impartial judgement. (Background/criminal records, age and gender). Both men had identical criminal records, were the exact same age, but differed in race and economic status; where the African American male came from an impoverished environment, where he grew up in a single parent home, had dropped out of junior high school and had held only two jobs in his entire life, the white male lived in an upstanding community, where his father was a well known business man and his mother was a nurse, he had graduated from college and was working as an intern at a big corporation. When they both appeared before the judge for sentencing, the scales of justice were definitely unbalanced. Both individuals had been arrested for possession with the intent to distribute fourteen grams of crack cocaine (or cocaine base), but received entirely different sentences. The African American male was given 120 months in federal prison, while the white male received drug treatment and 5 years probation. Reasoning as much as I could, there was no way that I was aloud to dispel the haunting feeling that I received from the disparity in the two sentences.

In your opinion was equality served or was injustice once again handed down to another member of a certain minority group, who most often find themselves at the blunt end of a judges gavel?

Mandatory or Mindless

Before mandatory sentence reform, did you know that; Karen Shook served over 10 years on a 20 to 40 year sentence of conspiracy to deliver and delivery of 50-224 grams of cocaine, before being released in 2003.

Angelita Able served over 10years on a 20 to 60 year sentence on one count each of delivery and conspiracy to deliver 225-629 grams of cocaine…

- In the state of Michigan, over 1,200 people were serving decades under mandatory sentences involving 650 grams of heroin or cocaine, Possession or delivery charges were routinely passed with conspiracy charges; doubling already harsh sentences. Low level drug offenders were often sentenced to serve lifetime probation or parole… In these instances, I ask you, is it morally or ethically correct to govern a man/woman for the rest of his/her life? You be the judge…

Justice Allah March,

2003 Brooklyn,

New York

If These Prison Walls Could Talk, what would they say?...

From the vast amount of time I've spent behind these prison walls, the many trials and tribulations I've overcame has given me a good understanding on confined behaviors. Observing my surroundings, just like one of the many cameras on these walls. Everyday life seems like a major sitcom or soap opera…

If These Prison Walls Could Talk, would they speak about the politics that it takes to keep a prison filled or built? Most prisons are built in a wilderness and the towns are developed rapidly to accommodate the institution. Auburn Correctional Facility in Auburn, New York is a good example; a person can't have a prior felony to work in a prison, they don't have to be a college graduate or have a basic education. Most people employed in the facility are family related or have been referred by a longtime employee. Father, mother daughter and son are common officers or staff in these places.

If These Prison Walls Could Talk, would they speak about the fear factor inside of these walls? Would they talk about the staff members who are afraid of a prison riot or an out of control prisoner who could harm himself or others? Prisoners outnumber staff fifteen-twenty to one at times….Prisoners are afraid of a lot of different things, but many will never admit it. Fear of showing any signs of weakness is one of them. In all actuality, prisoners are afraid of things they can't control, such as what goes on with their loved ones, while they are away. Most of them find religion as a way to cope with their fears and turn all of their worries over to their higher power…

If These Prison Walls Could Talk, would they speak about all of the grown men, walking around without an education or any type of comprehension skills? Who feel as if they have to keep it "gangsta" or real. Who walk around, afraid to pick up a book to improve themselves. Who are quick to go and buy the latest pair of boots or sneakers to try to impress those who are thoughtlessly running around, doing the same thing. "**You want to hide something from someone, then put it in a book**. Would these prison walls talk about all of the valuable time that is wasted in front of the (idiot box) television, watching videos, reality shows, or some sort of other programs, where women are degrading themselves? Would they talk about all of the war stories that are glorified and changed each time they are told?..

If These Prison Walls Could Talk, would they speak about all of the gang members, so called "clicks" and other individuals who take orders from another grown man? Who lacked the love of a mother or father while growing up. Who never felt affection from their parents. Would they talk about the individuals who joined gangs for protection? Or what about those who ask themselves what their lives would have been like if only they had listened to that inner voice of reasoning; their fifth grade teacher, basketball coach, grandmother or even their girlfriend, whoever warned them not to go...Watch the company you keep...and that the streets doesn't love anyone...

If These Prison Walls Could Talk, would they speak about the different types of religions and demonstrations that go on inside of them? Would they talk about the people who turn their lives over to "Christ" or "Allah" to help them cope with their time?

If These Prison Walls Could Talk, would they speak about the many inmates who are inside, suffering from some type of traumatic health issue or ailment due to the cut back in medical funding from the government? Would they talk about the 18 month long waiting list to see the dentist? Or what about the $2.00 fee that must be paid in order for them to see the doctor?

If These Prison Walls Could Talk, would they speak about all of the so called "know it alls." The people who are quick to point out all of your faults and character defects, but are unable to recognize their own? Who are afraid to look in the mirror at themselves and make the same assessment that they give to everyone else?

If These Prison Walls Could Talk, they would have to say that music soothes the souls of the wildest animals. It has helped me make it through some of the most trying times.

If These Prison Walls Could Talk, they would say damn it, man!!! Was it all worth this?

Peace!..

Cause and Effort

Most people view crime as a natural response to the inequality arising from the competition inherent in a capitalist society. Opportunities to advance and better ones living conditions are more plentiful in certain sectors. The group with the most power in any society ensures their values, shape their behaviors and pass down cultural traditions. Actions which are in conflict with the dominant group are identified as rebellious or of the criminal nature. Social, economic status, religion, ethnicity, race, education and environment play a major role in how one is viewed by society. Crime is an inevitable effect that is caused by oppression and degradation. For the many minorities who find themselves at a disadvantage, because of an economic system that seems to have been designed to keep them subservient to the upper class or rich, prison becomes an unconscious choice. Segregated by cultural diversity, they claim violence and crime. Discrimination fuels their already mixed emotions about race related issues and causes them to defend their distorted way of thinking.

Social disorganization is another major cause that leads to the domino effect of crime and recidivism. In order for this fallibility to be reversed, "we" the people must join together, direct our heads of state and rebuild our society on true equality and reform...

Chapter Two
"Responsibility"

Please watch your step as we enter cell Block-B; "**Responsibility**"; for those of you who have been irresponsible in your actions in the past, I ask that you abandon your old ways of thinking and allow yourselves to look at life from a new perspective…Take a walk with me to the rear of the unit where we will visit cell-115. Inside, we find inmate "1906067" "**Irresponsibility**."

- Websters Dictionary defines Irresponsible as; not responsible.

As irresponsibility reflects back over its life, it is constantly reminded of the devastation that being irresponsible has rendered to its very existence. Surrounded by four walls, there is no way to escape from dealing with the matter of thought. As pressing as the issue may be for the need to look within ones inner self, many individuals try their best to evade the confrontation. In doing so, valuable time is wasted, lessons that should have been taught by lifes never ending school of hard knocks are tossed aside, and the chance to move forward and advance is trampled upon for a safe haven of falsities and an unscrupulous way of thinking.

What happens to the individual who never searches for resolution in a dead sea of irresponsibility? When do the shores of responsibility connect to the docks, so that the wayward ships that they have been so aimlessly sailing upon may offer a place of refuge and sanctity? You must be honest with yourself; some of us will never make it. Will you be one of them?

If These Prison Walls Could Talk, they would commend TD Jakes for his visit to San Quentin Maximum State Prison, where he spent an entire night with some of the worlds most dangerous criminals. If these walls could talk, they would tell how men on death row were asking for prayer and slipping him notes. How through his ministry, men who had lived irresponsibly all their lives were repenting for their sins and were now willing to be held accountable for their past actions. **If These Prison Walls Could Talk**, they would also tell the story of how, while TD Jakes ministered to the prisoners that they were also ministering to him. They would tell how although all of the evidence of your wrong doing is right before you and how man will always make you pay, that "God" makes you just through forgiveness. **If These Prison Walls Could Talk**, they would go on to explain how TD Jakes explained to the men how he couldn't get them out of prison, but how he could help set them free. How unforgiveness keeps you chained to the past and that if you are unable to learn the art of forgiveness that you are destined to die by yourself. **If These Prison Walls Could Talk**, they would tell how you don't have to be behind bars to be imprisoned; but how you can be imprisoned by guilt, irresponsibility, chains from the past, drugs, gambling, adultery, alcohol, the streets and many other crippling vices that make forgiveness a life long process. **If These Prison Walls Could Talk**, they would tell of the dreams of one day when the liars would join hands with the hypocrits, judges would join hands with the drug dealers. The DA's would have mercy on the murderers, and the jurors would pray and ask "God" for guidance before finding the accused defendant guilty. **If These Prison Walls Could Talk**, they would champion responsibility and mourn out loud for those whose actions claim to be irresponsible...

Product Of Your Environment

How many of you have ever heard the cliché' **"Product Of Your Environment?"** Well, that is a widely used term, that is often only looked at in a negative way. No matter what type of environment you may have been born into, there is always a choice to what type of product that you can become. Did you know that as a youth, Judge Greg Mathis dropped out of school, and was sent to jail for nine months for carrying a gun? Although he had been raised in the same type of crime infested neighborhoods that many of you come from, he made a decision to overcome his bleak circumstances by educating himself. After obtaining his G.E.D., he went on to college and became the fine example of a man that many people turn to for guidance and advice.

Other individuals who have made the same type of conscious choices after having brushes with the law are; Charles S. Dutton (Rock), Vinge Raimes, Kareem 'Biggs' Burke, Warren Boyd, Errol Craig Sull, Akon, Allen Iverson, Markey- Mark, Maino, Emory Jones, Roscoe Ruiz,, Paul Fauteck, and Bernard Hopkins just to name a few.

Some social disorganization theories propose that negative crime rates are largely the result of poverty, urban decay and social disorder. They insist that because of the breakdown of health, urban communities are a major cause of criminal behavior. The lack of strong, family bonds, positive role models and an increasing unemployment rate also contribute to individuals becoming negative products of their environments. Other studies show that although not as common as in urban communities, this is also true in some rural areas. It must be noted that criminals do not come in one shade or color, but all share a distorted way of thinking. As all of the aforementioned individuals have shown; despite the circumstances that you may have been born into, or your present situation, at the end of the day, you are the one who decides what type of product you become.

Upstairs, on the second tier of cell block-B, lets' stop for a while at cell 2- 11, where "No Hope and Despair" have been sentenced to a life of unnecessary pain and lost love. As we examine the conditions surrounding their circumstances, we must take into account how the prison system claims to support the strengthening of family ties, but on the contrary only seems to destroy them.

Having just returned from a visit with his loved ones "No Hope" recounts how he and his family were mistreated by prison guards. He goes into how his wife and two children were verbally disrespected, unruly handled while being pat searched and asked to leave early because of overcrowding, after having driven over nine hours to get to the institution. If that hadn't been bad enough, neither of his sons had been permitted to sit on his lap, he was only allowed to briefly embrace his wife, and he had been threatened with termination of visiting privileges for being accused of challenging the correctional officers authority. Instead of feeling a sense of joy from having just seen his family, "No Hope" is weighed down with frustration and grief. Further strain had been added to an already complicated situation, driving a deeper wedge between him, his wife, and his two children. If they are unable to endure the blatant disrespect, and mistreatment provided by the prison staff, it won't be long before the visiting process is abandoned and their relationships begin to deteriorate at a faster rate.

As we turn our attention to "Despair", who is sitting at a metal desk, we notice that he is reading some sort of letter. After much coaxing, he finally shares it with us.

Some Women Wait…Some Don't!..

By Jaki McCalvin

Going back and forth to the prisons during the icy cold of the winter or the fiery heat of the summer can get overwhelming. Crowds of women and children are waiting to board the same bus as I am. All of us are tired and not looking forward to the long ride ahead.

But after I am seated on the bus, I let out a long sigh. I push back my seat. As the ride begins, I reflect on something that makes it all worth it. What is it?

I am thinking about my husband, but not how much I love him, not something he may have said or done, I am thinking about how much he has grown and matured since he walked into prison almost five years ago. I am thinking about the man I see in him today. He is 100% different from the man he used to be.

He is no longer confused, tormented by drugs and easily lured into the world of the criminal-minded. He is strong focused and confident. His newly found faith in "God" has contributed to his change. His faith also helps him survive prison life.

I see my husbands' changes not in the things he says or the dreams he writes about in his letters. Words can convince anybody of anything…Talk Is Cheap.

My husbands' growth and maturity, and how he is staying out of trouble, are in his works that are no longer filled with hatred and foul language. I see it in the way he is always trying to uplift others and tries hard to help someone, if he can.

I also see my husbands growth and maturity in the books he reads, and the fact that he does more than play cards and lift weights with his time. He has learned that all situations, both good and bad, can be used as opportunities to better himself.

One reason I notice these changes is that I look for them. To me, the worst thing is to be waiting for a man who, deep inside, I know hasn't changed, one bit.

Because there lies a strong chance that when he's back on the streets, he will do something that will land him right back in prison. Then all of my sacrifices will have been a waste of time.

I hurt for women who love men like this. I see the sadness in their eyes, and I hear them complain on the bus after a visit, that their man won't stay out of trouble long enough for them to enjoy a conjugal visit. They complain about having to deal with men who are too demanding and constantly complain. Because of that, women often leave a visit wishing they had never wasted their time and effort.

Malcom X once said, "To have been a criminal is not a disgrace, but to remain a criminal, that is the disgrace."

I am glad the criminal mentality is no longer a part of my husband. It reassures me that my time is not being wasted. Chances are high that he will come home and stay home. Now I take him seriously and have the respect for him I didn't have years ago. He has earned that respect. I pray for my sisters who aren't as fortunate as I am. They have to deal with husbands who have forgotten how to show love and appreciation for the things these women have done for them week after week. It takes a special kind of person to want a man in prison. It takes a love that many people find hard to understand, and often make fun of.

But, because of the love, we look past what people say and think. We asked that we are loved, respected and appreciated in return; and that they stay out of trouble. We also ask that they show interest in issues we want to discuss, and not just think that because they are in jail, they must be on the receiving end of everything.

As the wife of an inmate, I deal with other inmate wives and girlfriends, regularly. I know that a woman will stand by an incarcerated man if she sees growth and change in him. Those positive changes will cause her to feel her man is on the right track, and she no longer has any reason to worry.

She can therefore find peace, and her love for him will get stronger, instead of weaker.

If he is doing the right thing, he won't have to spend too much time worrying about his woman, either. Because; Take it from a woman, who knows – she ain't going nowhere…

Being one of those unappreciative husbands that Jaki McCalvin wrote about, it is evident why "Despair" has such a (bleak) outlook when it comes to his situation. Not only is he too busy feeling sorry for himself, and blaming everyone else for his poor decision making, he is doing nothing at all to better himself. Until he wakes up, takes responsibility for his actions, and realizes that he must change his way of thinking before he will ever be able to better his conditions, he will continue to be the guest of honor at his own pitty party. Failure will be his greatest gift, and a life of misery and loneliness will be his only companions…

>>>>>>>>>>>>>>>>>>>>>>>>>>>>>

Who's Going To Raise The Children?

This analysis is done according to Erikson's 8 Stages of Psychosocial Development:

Stage	Ages	Description
Trust vs Mistrust	Birth to 1 year	Infants learn to trust or mistrust depending on the degree and regularity of care, love and affection provided by parents or caregivers
Autonomy vs Shame and Doubt	1 to 3 years	Children learn to express their will and independence, to exercise some control and to make choices. If not, they experience shame and doubt.
Initiative vs Guilt	3 to 6 years	Children begin to initiate activities, to plan and undertake tasks, and to enjoy developing motor and other abilities. If not allowed to initiate or if made to feel stupid and considered a nuisance they may develop a sense of guilt.
Industry vs Inferiority	6 years to puberty	Children develop industriousness and feel pride in accomplishing tasks, making things and doing things. If not encouraged or if rebuffed by parents and teachers, they may develop a sense of inferiority.
Identity vs Role Confusion	Adolescence	Adolescents must make the transition from childhood to adulthood, establish an identity, develop a sense of self and consider a future occupational identity. Otherwise, role confusion can result.

Stage	Ages	Description
Intimacy vs Isolation	Young Adulthood	Young adults must develop intimacy–the ability to share with, care for, and commit themselves to another person. Avoiding intimacy brings a sense of isolation and loneliness.
Generativity vs Stagnation	Middle Adulthood	Middle aged people must find some way of contributing to the development of the next generation. Failing this, they become self-absorbed and emotionally impoverished and reach a point of stagnation.
Ego Integrity vs Despair	Late Adulthood	Individuals review their lives, and if they are satisfied and feel a sense of accomplishment, they will experience ego integrity. If dissatisfied, they may sink into despair.

As we take a look at the chart above, let us understand that without the proper love, affection, nurturing and guidance from a parent or care giver it is very difficult for a child to make the proper transition into adulthood. So many people underestimate the importance of instilling certain morals and values in their children at a young age. The absence of certain ingredients is most likely a recipe for disaster. When a child is left unattended, to figure out many of the things that he or she should be shown, their ineptness to make distinctions in a world far more advanced than their mental development will allow them to grasp leads to a sequence of repercussive decisions.

Many of the men that I've talked to in prison, over the years were unable to see how they had abandoned their responsibilities and left their children to a destitute fate; one that could and most likely would affect their families for generations to come. Without being given the proper instructions, the young boy or girl carries their mischievous ways over into adolescents. Having gone through childhood with aimless intent, they begin to search for an identity. Confusion sets in and further bad choices are made. If there is no interference to correct this misguided behavior criminal records and lengthy prison sentences are their rewards for being insolent. Having been robbed of a fair chance at life, by a parent, who never understood the astounding impact of not being presented with a positive role model to fashion their lives after they find themselves behind bars during their middle adulthood stage. During that time, if the much needed past reflections aren't initiated as a tool for growth and development, they will most likely descend into late adult hood, in bitterness and despair.

In many of the cases, many of the children would have had children, and left their children in the same or worse marred juncture. This cataclysmic cycle has been allowed to continue on for centuries, and only seems to be desecrating more with time. As we evaluate this situation and take the necessary steps in securing a brighter future for those to come after us, selfishness must be castigated and selflessness enthroned.

Who's Going To Raise The Children? Case in point; I read an article in The Patriot News, a few years ago, entitled "Guns and Drugs Star In Harrisburg Web Video: It was written by Tom Bowan. In the article, he writes about how a half dozen young men were in a video, on an Allison Hill street corner, posing with guns and what appeared to be crack cocaine. They were bragging about selling drugs and doing time in prison. The web video, which aired on You Tube caught the eyes of the authorities, often links were sent to the Patriot News and other media sites. Most of the participants, who had been on either parole or probation were immediately sent to jail. One of the youth boasted about being out of prison on bail and how he had been arrested for selling drugs. He goes on to say how he' is going to do his time and come back out and do the same thing.-Staring into the camera, in a close-up shot, his senseless talk leads to his daughter and how he proclaims that "She's gonna' be doin' coke wit' my homies, down here."

As I continued to read the article, in dismay, my heart was saddened. I began to contemplate on what would become of these young mens future and how they had no idea of the effects that one bad decision could have on their lives. Becoming angry, I thought about their parents. Where were they and how could they allow such an embarrassing thing to happen? Who was the real blame for this inane act that was reared in ignorance. Is it the father? Is it the mother? Or is it the entire community that turned its back, locked its doors, and refused to hear the silent cries of our most precious dying breed?

Having once been a disobedient child, in the school of experience, I've outgrown the over coat of delinquency, and garnered myself in responsibility. Earnest self-examination provided me with the insight to be able to step outside of the darkened shadows of illegality that had hindered me from becoming the man that I am today. Now that I am able to stand erect, undeviated by a troubled past, I ask myself, "Who's Going To Raise The Children?

A Race to Incarceration

Over the last three decades, the U.S. prison population has sweltered in size, despite attempts at commutation and criminal justice reform. Since the mid 1970's, the incarceration rate has quadrupled. Many African American males, ages 20 to 29 are under some sort of correctional supervision; whether it be probation, parole, county jail, state or federal prison. It has also been noted that nearly 7% of black children has an incarcerated parent.

In many of the inner-city neighborhoods across the country, an increasingly high number of African American males are laidened with criminal records. Binded by a system that preaches reform, but irrigates punishment, there is often times no room for rehabilitation. Funding for programs have been cut and there are little to no means for an individual to educate himself. Understanding the system the way that I do, I say this to those of you who may find yourself in what may seem a bleak and hopeless situation; take it upon yourself to learn whatever it is that you may need to know in order for you to be able to stop your world from continuing to revolve in a disastrous tail spin. "Without sacrifice, there will never be progress." Surround yourself with people who are trying to accomplish something in their lives and become a liberated student of change. Learn the value of a book and treasure the priceless information that you are able to extract from its contents. Knowledge is the only true power that can elevate a race from an existing and ever increasing mental state of poverty. Though opposition may arise during your quest for a better way of living, never allow yourself to waiver during battle. In the midst of the arena, you will discover that nothing can defeat a man who is saddled with determination. For it is his forth right once purpose and responsibility has been joined together in matrimony. Just as a people without vision is destined to perish; so a race that refuses to educate itself is bound for incarceration; be it mental or physical.

In reverence to Dr. Martin Luther King, Jr.'s birthday, I ask that you take a walk with me down to the prison chapel; where I once rendered this soul-stirring speech on January 13, 2011. At FCI Ray Brook.

I began; *Plead my cause O'Lord with those that stand with me. Fight against those that fight against me.*

"As I stand here before you tonight, honored to be a speaker at this more than memorable gathering, I have one question that I want to pose to

*all of you who are assembled together, out in the audience – **What War Are you Fighting?...** Do you stand on the same battlefield as Marcus Mosiah Garvey, Martin Luther, Malcom X, Booker T. Washington, Frederick Douglas, Ralph Waldo Emerson, Hue P. Newton and countless others who have fought and died so that you could have a better life? Or do you insist on running the concrete jungles with shameless drug dealers, mass murderers, gang bangers, hustlers, extortionist, false practitionists', con artist, thieves and pimps, who continue to destroy and disseminate all of the hard work that was built on the blood, sweat and tears of our forefathers?.. – Again, I ask, **What War Are You Fighting?..** Almost four hundred years ago, in 1712, a slave owner named Willie Lynch delivered an atrocious speech, on the banks of the James River. In the colony of Virginia... His speech was so masterfully and cunningly oratated that the effects of his poisonous words are still felt today! Although the shackles and chains have been removed from our bodies in the physical form, most of us remain trapped mentally, in iron clad.... Something far more detrimental than being forced into servitude. – Aware of the astounding effects that the power of thought has over man, Willie Lynch devised a diabolical plan that would segregate and annihilate... Playing chess, like only a real chess master would, he carefully strategized his moves light years ahead... - This malefic consortium even went as far as to dominate us in religion... - Take a look around... no matter the color, we are all one. But due to the venomous seed that had been planted in the minds of many of our ancestors, we now have the misconception that; "I'm from DC., Joe, I'm from Boston, I'm from New York, Sun, I'm from Jersey, I'm from Baltimore, Slim, I'm from Cook City, cuz, I'm from Philly, Roady, I'm from Pittsburgh,Brah, I'm from down south, dawg, I'm from Connecticut, I'm form the west coast and so on and so on; and if you ain't where I'm from, and it goes down, I'm poppin' ya' top!... – Looking at that statement from a conscious mans' point of view, I can only think to myself how lost we are as a people... - Again, I ask, **What War Are You Fighting?...***

I can remember vividly, almost twenty-two years ago, when I was a young boy, doing my first bid in the penitentiary; I met a man who would eventually help shape and mold me into the person that I am today... Not without a few bumps, bruises, costly losts and many trials and tribulations, though. Governed by inexperience and a lack of understand, I would often shun his wisdom and continue on in my foolish ways. – One day, while walking the track, me and Brother Darryl Ford, who was at the time doing a double life sentence, removed his dark shades and implored me, "look into my eyes and understand that I am your mirror! Change your ways or end up like me!" At the time, I was unable to comprehend to exactly what it was that he was trying to get me to see. Today, after having gone down many rocky roads, tripping, scraping my knees, and pulling myself back up, I now possess that quality of decision making that he had so earnestly tried to instill in me *as a youth. – Look at the man who is sitting or standing next to you.... No matter where he may be from, he is your mirror and you are his reflection... - Understand!*

*One final time, I ask you, **What War Are You Fighting?...** As I leave you with that thought, I want you to remember that you are the gateways to your childrens' futures... If you insist on continuing in the same fashion that lead to your incarceration, then you might as well write the very judge who sentenced you and ask him or her to lock your sons and daughters up, too!.. – Without your protection, providence and guidance, your family is lost! Destined for destitute... - Most of us robbed our wives of a husband, abandoned our kids, denounced our sisters; discarded responsibility and brought shame to our parents' names!... If that wasn't bad enough, we even caused mayhem and destruction throughout our communities... - Tonight, I call on you men to stand up and be accounted for! Let your voices be heard and your actions as one, who will be a part of the solution instead of part of the problem... We are only as strong as our weakest link! – For any man who is in search of peace, I advise you to prepare for war!"*

Thank You!

.

"The ultimate measure of a man is not where he stands in moments of comfort and convenience, but where he stands at times of challenge and controversy."

Dr. Martin Luther King, Jr.

A Broken Society

As I look around at the world that we live in today, it is far different that the one we lived in when I was a child. In many ways, from the top of the socioeconomic ladder to the bottom, we seemed to have become morally and ethically corrupt. A once loving, bright spirited and harmonious society has turned cold hearted, uncaring and tyrannical. The lawyers and judges play games of favors with human lives, the politicians preach change, but bring more of the same. The bankers and brokers steal more than they ever have before, the police thirst for brutality, many of the prisons are modern day slave camps and the citizens are like naïve sheep being lead to the slaughter. Whether you are a murderer or a white-collar criminal; in my eyes, it is all the same; the failure to love one another. We claim to have adopted religion, but cast down "Godly" ways without proper principles as the foundation, it is impossible for a people to govern themselves. Therefore, authority must be placed over them, and as history has told the daunting tales over and over again of those who have unjustly enslaved those who were of a social economic status, it continues to repeat itself. Is it me or does it seem like we live in an age where people have no regard for human life?

Our society is broken. We are the only ones who can fix it. In order for us to do so, we must learn to distinguish error from truth. Step outside of the shadows of darkness, into the light. We must wipe away the blinding tears of anguish and injustice, clothe ourselves in righteousness and stand for equality. We must learn the lessons that were handed down to us, teach our children a better way and never again allow ourselves to be controlled by power and corruption.

Just Another Number

Lance Williams

When Mr. Dolphin Discussed the concept and nature of why this book was being written, I felt honored to be a part of something of such magnitude. Having researched the stats of parity between black men, women and our youth compared to other ethnic groups, it was essential as another black man, who is incarcerated to express my unbiased views on what I see as modern day slave camps.

My name is Lance Williams, I am currently serving an eleven and a half years sentence, for aiding and abetting prostitution across state lines. Instead of being censored as a member of society, I am now an eight-digit number, who is censored by the Federal Correctional Institution of the government of the United States of America. I have been separated from my family, I am no longer allowed to vote, and I am no longer a part of the continued production of our race. I don't blame the bigotry or racism that still exists today for my incarceration, I blame myself. The choices that I made played a major part in me becoming a part of the problem that continues to plague our society. Having grown up in the urban sections of Boston Mass or "The Ghetto", which is a word to me that sounds degrading and stereotypes our people to critical judgement, I was raised along with four other brothers by a strong, black single woman. She protected, nurtured and provided for us, while the men who had helped bring us into this world were either incarcerated or too caught up in the street life to accept their responsibilities. Our house wasn't much different than any other homes in the neighborhood. It seemed natural for me to go over to my friend's house and see a single mother raising her children as well. The odds of a father being present was slim to none.

Coming from a long line of hustlers, drug dealers, con-artist and pimps, from the north shore, along with having a father who had been imprisoned for most of my life, it is sad to say that the apple didn't fall far from the tree. Like so many other black youth, I had been born into "The Game." I senselessly dropped out of high school in the 8th grade. At the time I didn't have any idea of how much of an important role school played in me becoming a productive member of society. Blindly, I wanted my education to come from the streets, so I emulated what I saw in the people who were around me. I wanted the fast money, fancy cars and loose women. Too young to realize that it was all just a façade that came with a bleak future, I jumped in with both feet. I didn't understand that it was considered lucky to end up where I find myself today. Some of the people that I grew up with weren't as fortunate. Many of them died from street violence, some sort of disease or are now strung out on the very drug in which they once sold.

Finding no sense of glorification in the lifestyle that I once lived, I realize that it was only a deception of what I thought would lead to a better future. Better choices would have definitely taken me in a different direction. In retrospect, I feel that it is a must that we do more to touch base with our youth. Let us find out what they need to help them feel as though their lives are worth living. Equipped with more positive role models and sound advice that they feel that they can use for their betterment, they are more prone to beat the odds. We have come a long way as people, but there is much more road for us to travel. Our ancestors sacrificed their lives so that we could have a brighter future. From the treacherous ship rides, where we had been kidnapped from our mother land; to the White House, where a black man was elected president, let us stand for something, or continue to fall for nothing.

I feel that if every black man and woman takes our youth and gives them some good orderly direction, we will one day be able to change the disturbing stats of our people being at the top of the list when it comes to us occupying the these modern day slave camps. But until that happens, we will continue to be "just another number."

One day, while working as an orderly on the unit, I was cleaning an empty cell, when I found an unaddressed,opened envelope with a letter inside. The person who wrote it had never sent it out to the intended party. Touched by the words that had been written, I felt compelled to share it with you.

Dear friend,

I'm writing to say thank you for making my faith in the Lord stronger, because of the things that you do not do. Like when I look for a letter from you, that never comes, "He" then assures me of the fact that "His" word contains love letters, which are capable of calming my aching soul.

Or like when I yearn for you to visit me, if for nothing else but to provide me with a much needed hug, and you never show up. "HE" then comforts me by reminding me of all of the times "HE" has shown up to comfort me in my most deepest times of need.

Or during the times when I've called, and you were not at home to receive my calls; even the times when you were home, but refused to pick up the receiver. "HE" then whispers in my heart words of wisdom that lets me know beyond a shadow of a doubt, that "He'll" answer my every call.

I am also reminded of the times when you did answer my calls, only to make promises that you knew you had absolutely no intentions of keeping. "He" then affirmed to me in ways that truly amazed me; that all of "His" promises towards me are YES and AMEN.

You see, by neglecting to actually demonstrate your professed love for me, I've been allowed to see just how much "He" truly loves and cares for me. So, I thank you for the neglect and apathy that you've so very, relentlessly demonstrated towards me. I also appreciate your lack of support for me. Where you've failed to aid and assist me in accomplishing my many goals, that I've been striving to fulfill, despite my apparent limitations.

Had you performed any of the many facets of true love toward me, I would not have on my own realized just how much the "Lord" truly loves and cares for me. As it is written; ***A man that has friends must show himself friendly!.. And there is a friend that sticks closer than a brother. (Prov. 18:24) When my father and my mother forsake me, then the Lord will take me up… (Psalms 27:10) At my first answer, no man stood with me, but all forsook me; I pray to "God" that it might not be laid to their charge. Not withstanding the Lord stood with me and strengthened me…(2-4:16)***

True love requires sacrifice. It commands action. It also demonstrates compassion, provides comfort and produces support. Especially under extreme circumstances. For love is the effectual antidote to the agonizing trauma caused by loneliness, stress, depression and despair.

Love, therefore, never fails, for its power is as strong as death itself; meaning that it is fully capable of having a permanent effect upon the life of the one it has been demonstrated towards. As such love always seeks another's wellbeing, is exceptionally kind, forgiving and cannot be quenched by mere circumstances or conditions…Love truly endures.

Yet, one must possess love before one can effectually demonstrate love. For love transcends the very words that proceeds out of our mouths. Its origin is from "God", who has graciously deposited "His" love into the lives of those who have put their trust in "Him". Amen and Amen.

Please make no mistake about it. I love you, not because you deserve it. No, not at all, but because you need to be loved. And I long for the day when I'll be able to effectually demonstrate my love for you, without any barriers standing in-between us.

Forever

Your

Friend

p.s.

    If "HIS" love is truly in you, then please do demonstrate that love towards those with whom you may come in contact with. Because not everyone will be able to grow closer to the Lord through your unwillingness to demonstrate the love "He" has placed within your heart.

Responsibility

Earl Scott

This is a story about four people, named; Everybody, Somebody, Anybody, and Nobody.

There was an important job to be done, and Everybody was sure that Somebody would do it. Anybody could have done it, but Nobody did it. Somebody got angry about it, because it was Everybody's job. Everybody thought Anybody could do it, but Nobody realized that Everybody wouldn't do it. It ended up that Everybody blamed Somebody, when Nobody did what Anybody could have done…

Excerpt from:

Message In The Music

Chapter Three
The Past

The next ward of the prison is called C-Block. This unit is where the inmates are mentally stuck in the past, refuse to change, and continue to blame everyone else for their current predicament. So enthralled in anger, self-pity, revenge and unbridled hate for authority, they have unconsciously allowed themselves to be chained to a life time of bitterness and drudgery. Unaware of the consequences of their morbid train of thoughts, they impassively continue to waste the valuable time that they were given to fully reexamine themselves, find out exactly who they are and how they ended up in such a dilemma.

Inside of cell-116, on the first tier, we find two inmates, engaged in a conversation. One is listening, while the other is shaking his head. Both are enraged by the lengthy amount of time that the courts had given them. Neither can see what part they played in the entire set-up. Unable to grasp the larger scope of things, they fume about how unjust the system is. How accurately that may be at times that still doesn't excuse the unlawful acts that they abided in. Their criminal pasts, along with a sordid way of thinking is what ultimately lead to their current state of incarceration. In order for either of these two individuals to understand this, they must free themselves of past debaclements, cease from playing the blame game, and search diligently for a solution. But, first the admittance of a problem must be addressed.

Are you aware that negative thinking can be a disease? Not in the form of a physical ailment, but in a mental malady. If allowed to penetrate the mind and fester, negative thoughts can and has immobilized entire races of people. The masterfully woven template of psychological dis-empowerment that was brought forth by Willie Lynch is a perfect example. By planting a seed of dissociative disorder in the minds of the people, he was somehow able to calculate the staggering foregone conclusion that we see today. Whether a physical slave or a mental slave, the main subjection of certain conditions are catastrophic to those who find themselves ensnared by the overbearing influence. As I share pieces of Willie Lynchs' speech with you, take a look around and see if his words rang true:

Gentlemen, I greet you here, on the banks of the James River, in the year of our Lord, one thousand, seven hundred and twelve (1712). First, I should thank you, the gentlemen of the colony of Virginia, for bringing me here. I am here to help you solve some of your problems with your slaves. Your invitation reached me on my modest plantation in the West Indies, where I have experimented with some of the newest and still the oldest methods of controlling slaves. Ancient Rome would envy us if my tactics are implemented.

As our boat sailed south, on the James River, named after our illustrious King, whose version of the Bible we cherish, I saw enough to know that your problem is not unique. While Rome used cords of wood, and crosses for standing human bodies along its highways, in great numbers, you are here, using the tree and the rope. By your methods, you are not only losing valuable stock, but you are creating uprises. Slaves are running away, your crops are sometimes left in the field too long for maximum profit, you suffer occasional fires and many of your animals are killed.

Gentlemen, you know what your problems are; I do not need to elaborate. I am not here to enumerate your problems, I am here to introduce you to a method of solving them. I have in my bag here, a full-proof method for controlling your slaves. I guarantee everyone of you that if applied correctly, it will control the slaves for at least three hundred years!

I have outlined a number of differences among the slaves; and I take these differences and make them bigger. I use fear, distrust, and envy for control purposes...

Distrust is stronger than trust, and envy stronger than adulation, respect or admiration. The slaves, after receiving this indoctrination shall carry on and will become self-refueling and self-generating for hundreds of years, maybe even thousands.

Don't forget that you must pitch the old, black male vs the young, black male, and the young, black male vs the old black male. You must use the dark skin slaves vs the light skin slaves, and the light skin slaves vs the dark skin slaves. You must use the female vs the male, and the male vs the female. You must also have white servants and overseers, who distrust all blacks. But, it is necessary that your slaves trust and depend on us!

Gentlemen, these kits are your keys to control. Use Them! Have your wives and children use them! Never miss an opportunity! If used intensely for one year, the slaves themselves will remain perpetually distrustful. Thank you gentlemen...

Having been deemed successful on the black race, this method was expanded and used on other ethnic groups. Most notably today are the Mexicans. Who are known by many as the new Ni**A.

If you were to take a man, woman, or child, and place them in the most undesirable conditions, then train them to value their positions, after a while those conditions would become normal, as well as desirable. Prone to accept what has been distilled in them over a length of time, they will no longer aspire to live a better life. In so many aspects, Willie Lynchs' speech has been the catalyst to breaking down and distorting the human mind. No longer does the young respect the old; the old have no compassion for the youth. The man doesn't respect the woman. The woman doesn't respect herself, therefore she is unable to respect her man, and the child grows up in obscurity.

Crime, poverty, racism, and fallacious thinking has become a normal way of life for so many in the U.S. It is no simple matter to be able to determine the exact extent to which mass incarceration, hidden political agendas, and social economic status has discolored our communities. At every level, minorities are the victims of racial bias when it comes to the judicial system and being treated equally. Until we make a conscious effort to wake up, stand up, and clean up, the injustice that has been handed down to us for over four hundred years will continue to stifle the generations to come.

"If These Prison Walls Could Talk"

What Would They Say?...

I've seen what remains hidden
I've heard the outspoken words of silence
I've concealed and sheltered those who society
refuses to house....

I've harvested the truth of liars, but I didn't ask to be here...
I am bound
Just as those whom which I bind
Each day, they stare into the eyes of the condemned
none the wiser
That I am watching...

I've been bathed in blood
I've even taken part in assaults
That have gone unseen
I have the fingerprints of the guilty
I've seen death
I've witnessed rapes
I've been there when the keepers come to take
All of what little those whom which I house own....

If I could talk
The system would be afraid
of what I have to say
I know the truth....

Kenyon LaMonte' Williams

Aka

Infinite Paradox

Did you know that as of the writing of this book, that there are at least ten states that deny ex-felons voting right, for life? Many rule, 13% of all black men in the United States have lost their electoral rights. Due to past, bad decision making they continue to be punished for a debt that has already been paid. Along with many other obstacles that is being placed in front of ex-offenders to keep the recidivism rate at a high level, they are being denied access to extensive drug treatment, job training, cognitive behavior and educational programs. The government claims lack of funding. But I ask you; without treatment, training, cognitive development or education, where is the rehabilitation? One of the leading factors in mass incarceration is a lack of job skills, for disadvantaged people. In order to correct a system that is obviously not working, I feel that a greater percentage of the money that is being spent on incarceration should be allocated towards more drug programs, job training, cognitive dissonance and education of all kinds. For an ex-felon who returns to the streets, without any form of education or job skills, there is a real up-hill battle. And for those who are unable to receive the type of out-patient drug treatment, mentoring and counseling that they need in order for them to be able to cope with everyday life it is only a matter of time before they end up back in prison. **Understand**: When a person has been used to living a certain type of lifestyle, it is sometimes impossible for them to change. Just like a drug, lifestyles are often addictive. For those who are unable to break the chainz of old habits, incarceration becomes a norm. Three undesirable meals, a hard cot, and a luke warm shower is all they have to look forward to. Hours turn into days, days turn into months, months turn into years and years turn into decades. The present becomes the past and they continue to hold on to a weight that will forever hold them down.

Mental Chainz

In the 1950's, a famous psychologist, named Julian Rotter came up with a concept called the "Locus Of Control: The Locus of Control refers to an individuals perception about the underlying main causes of events in his/her life. They believe that their destiny is controlled by their internal efforts, thoughts and decisions, and by external forces; fate, luck, or other powerful forces.

Rotter bridged behavioral and cognitive psychology. His view was that behavior is largely guided by rewards and punishments; and that individuals come to hold beliefs about what causes their actions based on these contingencies. In their mind, if the reward outweighs the consequences, whether good or bad, they are willing to take whatever risks to get what they want. Their beliefs in turn, determine what types of attitudes and behaviors they adopt. – Unconsciously, many people chain themselves to a negative way of thinking.

Essentially, Rotter investigated how peoples behaviors and attitudes affected the outcome and conditions of their lives. Those who tend to dwell at the low end of the Locus Control spectrum will remain in mental chains. Those who choose to elevate their thinking and descend to the upper level of The Locus Control spectrum hold the key to an unrestricted process of free thought. –think positive, get positive results. Think negatively and negativity will be yours to own.

Will You Remain In Mental Chains?...

The $O.G.$ Wise Man

Did You Know that criminal justice policies are pushing hundreds of thousands of already disadvantaged minorities even further into poverty? No job skills = no work. When there is lack of work, the crime rate and poverty goes up…

If These Prison Walls Could Talk, would they remind us of the many young men who have left the confined gates of correctional facilities only to have their lives taken away once they've hit the streets?... –Allow a moment of silence, as we stop in front of cell-201. For five years, this is where 24 year old Oreon Beylin spent a majority of his time. Having grown up in one of the poorest sections of Akron, Oh, with a mother who was a crack addict, a father who was never around, and an older sister whom never seemed to care about his wellbeing, he began to get into trouble at a very young age. On his 12th birthday, he joined a gang. In search of someone who he felt would treat him like family, he became a part of The Bloods. By age 18, he had been to several youth homes, did a short stint in the county jail and was now doing five years in federal prison for possession of a fire arm. Although it was almost eight years ago, it seems just like yesterday when Oreon and I met. After he had arrived on the compound, one of his homeboys brought him down to the gym where I was working out and introduced us. The following day, I took him under my wing and began to train him. As our relationship grew, so did my care and concern. Seeing many of the things in him that I once saw in myself, I began to try and enlighten him on many of his misguided and darkened views. The lessons that I had learned from not paying attention when Brother Darryl had tried to school me when I was that very age, had shaped and molded me into the type of man that many of the prisoners respected. Having acquired a passion for trying to deter the youth from ending up like I did, I often found myself walking the yard, giving them what at one time was given to me. Unable to understand where I was headed back then, I did my best to open up their eyes and warn them of the trouble ahead. Few listened. Many didn't. Could I blame them? Had I listened? In Oreons case, although he held me in high regards in some areas, there were others where our ideologies continued to clash. I stayed on him about getting his G.E.D., the people he hung around and not allowing his past to continue to haunt him.- Over the years that he and I spent together in prison, he had matured, but there were just somethings that he was unwilling to let go of. Upon acquiring his G.E.D., I had a big party for him down in the recreation area, I shared his joy and we were both proud of his accomplishment.

When the time grew near for Oreon to go home, I again warned him about people, places and things. He assured me that whatever came his way, he would be able to handle. I wasn't convinced. From having studied his behavior, I could tell that he wasn't done with the street life. In some ways, I could see his future.

On the day of his release, he hugged me and promised to keep in touch. – Less than three weeks after Oreon was back out on the streets, he was murdered at a night club by another gang member. The tragic news shook me for a moment, but there was nothing that I could do. The past had robbed him of his existence and left me with only a few memories to hold on to.

Yesterday is gone….

What will become of tomorrow?...

The O.G. Wise Man

Chapter Four
"The Present/Confessions"

D-Block is one of the better units inside of the facility. Here, you will find many of the prisoners working diligently to free themselves from past restraints. Midway down the tier in cell 114, we find inmate William Bradley engulfed in his studies. He reads aloud from a manuscript called: "Message In The Music, which was written by Earl Scott and revised by Dr. Kevin E. Dolphin.

"What I see around me in here (within the prison industrial complex), on a daily basis, is a vast majority of individuals who have no sense of ethics, character, honor, responsibility... morality. There is no effort made to educate self. No effort made to curb self-instructive vices and traits. Future plans incorporate the needs of "Self", but tangentially the needs of their children, of their parents, of their communities, of their race. I live within the phenomenon of a soda commercial, "Image Is Everything."

To establish substance involves work, and work is hard; and therefore undesirable to many. So, when I read criticisms by our Black leaders, of the prison industrial complex, I expect to also read about some solutions to these problems. It is a simple request. This is the problem;... this solution is incorrect;... so, here is a better one. There has to be a solution ventured. I do not want many of these individuals returning to our communities with their avariciousness, their violence, their ignorance, and their destructiveness. Too many are no good to anything or anyone. Their children love them, their parents love them, their wives or girlfriends love them; but love is historically blind!

*That doesn't excuse our Black leaders in their misguidance. As Marcus M. Garvey says in **"Message To The People"**, "Nobody is obligated to you to make you, so don't carry your sorrow to the world on your sleeves. Keep them to yourself and get out of them the best way you can. Leaders are not children, they must not, therefore, act as children."*

I see what can almost be likened to a condition of "mass hysteria." For too many of our people are finding fault with "white people", or the government, for our negative social conditions. Blaming "white people" is a historical "knee jerk" reaction. It serves as our outlet for releasing some of the animosity held towards racism today, more so than towards slavery yesterday. Blaming the government is more complex.

True indeed, there is a lack of the human emotion of "caring" coming from the government towards us, but the government isn't a human entity! It is an institution. Most institutions, even those that like to claim otherwise, are basically uncaring. If you or I took someone in off the street, out of concern for them, we would do whatever we could do for that person –human to human. Institutions usually focus on one aspect. An institution may house them, may feed them, may clothe them, but there is no person to person empathetic connection. My point is, the institutions fulfilled their purposes, but they rarely get emotionally involved.

We point to the U.S. government and we seek to show that it has a policy of benign neglect towards us. We holler out, "why?!" I say, "stand back if you want, we can do for self!" No, I don't mean that we shouldn't lobby for what we are supposed to have coming. We must do that. I am only saying that if the government never gives us anything, we can still find for self. Actualization through our own initiative as a people. Others do. Yes, racism is our own specter, but we have always walked over it once we've gotten our feet moving. When you begin walking, you never know where you'll end up; but if you stand still, you'll most certainly always be where you are!

Laws should be clearly supportable, because they are protecting safeguards; but once any of them are clearly shown to be onerous to the developmental growth of sociality, in its interrelation aspect, then there should be resistance to the correction of this defect.

The primal fallacy at play, in this equation, is that identifying someone/something as being "bad" does not automatically confer eternal "good" status on someone/something else. Meaning that the victims of racism/racists are good. It simply means that they have been victimized. The personal character of the victim is a whole separate matter.

*Listen to Marcus M. Garvey again, from **"Message To The People"**, "Society is an organization of mankind to safeguard and protect its own interest. When society is organized and is made evident by regulations, rules and laws, every member of that society must obey the said rules, regulations and laws. Therefore, always live up to the organized system of the society of which you form a part. The only alternative to this is rebellion. You should never join rebellious movements against society, except when there is good reason and justification for it. Society is intended to maintain the greatest good for the greatest number; and that is always upper-most, so that in thought you may have to reform. Any society must be calculated to bring about the greatest good for the greatest number; and you must obey its laws. Otherwise, you are an evil genius, living in the midst of the society, and that* *society will seek to destroy you or compel you to obey its rules, regulations and laws. You cannot live by yourself in a society. You must live upon the good will of your fellow citizens. Therefore, in that society, you must respect everything that tends to the good of all."*

Malcom X (Al-Hajj Malik El-Shabazz) was a man for whom I hold much admiration and respect above and beyond that which should automatically be rendered to our Black leaders. He walked away from incarceration as a MAN!... And few do. His greatest legacy is his metamorphosis and his growth as a thinker and as a leader of his people. He never stopped questioning his positions, and weighing them against his objectives. Above all else, he was morally rooted. That fact brought about his separation from Elijah Muhammad. He could not blindly ignore his perception of a factual weakness in someone whom he considered a leader. I am a Black man. I look to Black men and Black women as my leaders, and as the leaders of my people. But, I cannot ignore factual weaknesses that may exist within them.

Refuse to confer lifelong leadership to someone because of their public speaking skills, or their having been involved in a renowned group, or their having authored a book, or their having written a song, or their having acted in a movie, or their prowess on the sporting field of play. A willingness to sacrifice for your people does not automatically translate into productive leadership.

As a current prisoner in the federal bureau of prisons, who has spent nearly half of my life locked away, I feel that I am adequately equipped to speak on this topic. I will admit that I am not a scholar; like Malcom X, my alma mater was books. But as Web Dubois says in **The Souls of Black Folk**, *"Honest and earnest criticism from those whose interest are most nearly touched, criticism of writers by readers of governments by those governed, of leaders by those led, this is the souls of democracy and the safeguard of modern society."*

The problem within has to exceed the problem without. How are you going to address it, my leaders? This is not a case of bad things happening to good people, and until it does become such, we need to concern ourselves with the needs of the whole, before the few. A growing percentage of our youth are ending up in the nations prison system. It would be better off if we looked upon them as we do the many dreadful images of starvation and death in Africa – with regret, but no sense of involvement. A sort of subliminal concession to natural selection.

Ask yourself, what it is that you are really seeking. Study history with an eye geared toward seeing how others have gained or lost, through their methods of struggle, and adjust accordingly....

>>>>>>>>>>>>>>>>>>>>>>>>>>>>>>>

If These Prison Walls Could Talk, would they inform the world on how the United States has the highest per capita incarceration rate in the world? And how one of the fastest growing sectors of the prison/industrial complex is private corrections companies. Would they talk about how American Express and General Electric have invested in private prison construction in Oklahoma and Tennessee? Or how Correctional Corporations of America, one of the largest, private owners already operate internationally with 48 facilities in 11 states, including Puerto Rico. Under contract by the government, they are paid a fix sum per prisoner to operate those jails and prisons as cheaply and efficiently as possible. These private owners are making billions of dollars by cutting corners and denying prisoners the proper treatment. Extreme overcrowding and a lack of skilled staff only add to the growing problem. When it comes to labor, the inmates can be forced to work for little or nothing. Why? Because by breaking the law, they gave up most of their rights. **If These Prison Walls Could Talk**, would they tell the story of Bob Barker, the owner of Bob Barker Company, Inc. for preying upon the minorities misfortunes when sent to prison, and how he owns everything from van cells, to bed sheets to tooth brushes, toothpaste and soap. **If These Prison Walls Could Talk**, what would they really say?...

Federal Growth Continues

Although claims are being made to the public about prison relief, the over- crowdedness on the inside continues to grow. The Federal prison population has grown at a much faster rate than has the state population; more than doubling since the mid 90's. Here's a few reasons why: The federal government takes over the majority of the state cases, where they see that a defendant may have a chance to beat the case in court. The federal system has tougher sentencing laws; they play by a whole different set of rules when it comes to jury selection, evidence, and admissible testimonies. They have more complex supervision polices and fewer opportunities for diversion when it comes to being convicted. The federal government has over a 90% conviction rate. Despite corrections cost almost quadruple and costing the tax payers billions of dollars each year over the past couple of decades, more prisons continue to be built. Corrections has been the second fastest growing category of many state budgets, behind only Medicaid...

On an average day, more than 5,700 inmates can be found occupying New Yorks federal prisons. That is far much more than the prescribed 3,600. According to certain sources, New Yorks four federal prisons are atleast 50% over capacity; with FCI Ray Brook leading the way; with well over 60%. With that type of over crowdedness, how is it possible for the inmates to receive proper rehabilitation and treatment.

System wide, it is said that federal prisons are operating at 37% above capacity. The average, however, disguises a large range; from a low of 10% over capacity in minimum security prisons to a high of 49% in high security facilities. The other two categories are low security prisons, which are between 32-35% over capacity and medium security institutions, which are at somewhere around 48% over capacity.

Another claim has also been made that the reason for over crowdedness in New Yorks federal prisons were because federal facilities make an effort to keep prisoners close to their home communities. Having spent nearly nine years in FCI Ray Brook, I know that to be misleading, first hand. At the time that I was sent to the prison, I lived in South Carolina. That is over a thousand miles away from my wife, children and grandchildren. I fought diligently to get close to my family, but each time, I was given a different reason as to why I had to remain at the institution. I also met hundreds of other inmates who were in the same predicament. Some were said to have been sent there for disciplinary actions, others for gang affiliation and others for bed space. FCI Ray Brook is not the only prison that this goes on in; it is happening in nearly every federal correctional facility in the country.

Overcrowding in the U.S. penal system is not surprising to many. America has the largest incarceration population in the world. We have almost one in every 100 adults behind bars. But persistently, it is touted as being the land of the free! With these type of conditions, I ask myself; is it?...

Brick Walls

I am a prison wall. I am made of brick. My reason for being built is to keep one group of people away from another group of people. You could categorize them as "good and bad." Since the day that my very first brick had been put into place, I have been doing exactly what I was built to do. I don't have a choice in the matter for which I stand for; but being built properly, with a firm foundation has allowed me to endure the changes of time. While many who would stand for nothing, I the wall won't fall for anything. I truly wish to confine no one, and if it was up to me, I wouldn't. But those whom I confine seem to fight to be confined by me.

I am a prison wall and I won't fall for nothing. Those who find themselves trapped inside of my bowels seem unwilling to stand for anything. **I am a prison wall...**

Shahad

Richard Allen Projects

Phila, Pa

If These Prison Walls Could Talk

According to the Philadelphia Inquire; 6/14/11

Ex-warden in Philadelphia Charged In Gun Cover Up.

A former prison warden in Philadelphia has been charged in a cover-up, involving a guard who brought a gun into the Federal Detention Center in Center city. A cover up story was created, which suggested that the guard had permission to bring the weapon inside, on August 30, 2010, because his trunk lock was broken, federal prosecutor said, Tuesday. If convicted of the charges, the ex- warden faces a prison term of up to 110 years, for obstruction, witness tampering and lying to authorities...AP Associated Press

With people such as the one that you just read about running our penal system, we must continue to push for reform. Not only on the inside.

As we visit with a couple of more inmates, who are in cell 208, we find them in a deep discussion about **"Rational and Irrational"** thinking.

- *It is very obvious that we are not influenced by facts", but by our own interpretation of the "facts". –Alfred Adler*

- *As a man thinketh, so is he...-The Bible*

- *Men are not worried by things, but by their ideas about things. When we meet difficulties, we become anxious or troubled. Let us not blame others, but rather ourselves, that is: our idea about things...Epictetus, somewhere around 60 AD.*

Our thoughts influence our feelings and actions. If you think that you are a failure, then most likely you will fail. If you think that your efforts will end in a disaster, then you will be reluctant to give your all. If you think that an honest day of hard work will never pay off, then short cuts, illegality, and crime will become a way of life for you.

What kind of ideas are irrational;that make us upset or "sick"? Ellen Harper (1975) described ten common irrational ideas, such as "everyone should love and approve of me", "I must be competent; it would be awful to fail", "when bad things happen, I am unavoidably very unhappy and should be", "It is terrible when things don't go the way I want", and so on...

There are hundreds of such ideas which transform, for some people, life's ordinary disappointments into terrible, awful, and catastrophic. Preferences that are quite reasonable are made in our minds into absolutely unreasonable shoulds, musts, and demands, which are very upsetting. Mole hills become mountains. We talk ourselves into emotional traumas; yet, the upset person thinks the external events, not his/her thoughts, are upsetting him/her. Ellis called this mental process "awfulizing" or "catastrophizing".

What is rational thinking? First, as Carolos Rogers said, "the facts are friendly". We must face the truth; that's rational. Secondly, if we view reality as a determinist, we will tell ourselves that "whatever happens is lawful, not awful". Everything has a cause(s). The connections (called laws) between causes and effects are inevitable; the nature of things. So when something happens that you don't like, don't get all bent out of shape, just accept that the event had its necessary and sufficient causes (and try to change it the next time). Thirdly, Ellis urges us to constantly use the scientific method of objective observations and experimentation; i.e. the systematic manipulating of variables to see what happens. For example, if you feel that no one will hire you, Ellis would give you an assignment to apply for five different jobs that you are qualified for. If you believe that no one would hire you proved to be correct with those five jobs, then Ellis would direct you to start manipulating the variables; e.g. How can your appearance, demeanor, presentation, and observing change the outcome. In short, we accept what is happening and what has happened as lawful, as the natural outcome of immutable but complex laws, and not as terrible, awful events that we or someone should have prevented. And while we can't change the past, we can learn to use the"laws of psychology" to help ourselves and others in the future. What we can't change in the future, we can accept.

To understand any strong, troublesome emotion, you need to see clearly the three parts of your experience:

1. The actual upsetting physical-social situation and event, what you and others did, and the outcome. Example: you and your girlfriend argued about what to do this evening, go to the movies or visit her family. She got her way.

2. The thoughts, wishful images, and self talk you had before, during and after the event, but especially before feeling bad. This includes what you had hoped would originally happen, and how you wished it had worked out. Example: She doesn't even consider the things I want to do. I know that we both would have enjoyed the movie. She always has to try to control our relationship. She is more into her family than she is into me. I don't think her father likes me, anyway. I sure hate missing the movie.

3. Your emotional reactions about or to the event, and the outcomes. Example: I feel frustrated when I try to communicate with her; I'm upset because it seems as if she never considers what I want to do; I resent her inconsiderateness. I don't know if getting married to her would be such a good idea.

But, without some instructions, we don't recognize that some of our thoughts (2) may be irrational or unreasonable. Therefore, the description of this method begins with a careful explanation of rational thoughts. Then, more rational thinking is described with these concepts in mind. It will be easier in step 3 for you to select either a troublesome emotion (3) or do upsetting situation (1), and then go looking for your irrational ideas and unfulfilled expectation that really produce your overly intense emotions.

-When trying to maintain a rational train of thought, remember that critical thinking is key....

- Critical thinkers do not automatically accept and believe what they read or hear. They carefully analyze and evaluate every situation, with a reasoning eye. They are able to recognize manipulative emotional appeals, spot unsupported assumptions and detect faulty logic.

- Critical thinkers are slow to pass judgement or jump to conclusions. They are prone to looking at the other persons feeling and needs, as well as their own.

- Critical thinkers are never bound by past judgements or beliefs. They never allow selfish desires or wants to play any part when it comes to their decision making.

"The Walls"

You ask me what it's like here…

Using words, it's very hard to describe…

It's painful…

Lonely…

And often hard to deal with…

Men/women often go mad…

They lose all sense of direction…

They die an endless death…

They are reborn each day…

Just to die again…

Inside the madness of "THESE WALLS"…

The O.G. Wise Man

Come along, as I invite you to the chapel again, at FCI Ray Brook, where I delivered another uplifting speech; after graduating as a credentialed alcohol and substance abuse counselor (CASAC).

July 9, 2010

Good morning. (pause)

As I stand here before you today; a chosen voice of the class of 2010 CASAC graduates, I would like to thank the Warden, Associate Warden, Mr. Delgado, Mrs. Macy and all other faculty members for their insurmountable efforts to make sure that this esteemed program remains active within the institution. Being one of so many who have been fortunate enough to benefit from the therapeutic knowledge that is professionally and carefully administered, I want to convey to all of you just how much you are valued and appreciated. (pause)... the class of 2010 CASAC graduates would also like to thank Mrs. Gay, Mr. Onni, Mr. Ammel and Ms. Reom. Although Mrs. Gooden and Mr. Kaliza are unable to be here and share in this monumental moment with us, our thanks and gratitude goes out to them, as well...(pause)

Before I continue, I would like to say that all of the men who are embodied here with me in this room are more than qualified to present this speech. In fact, I feel that I am the least qualified. Without the support of my constituents, I doubt if I would be in this position. (Each one teach one) (short pause)... Throughout my long walk on this journey that we call life, I've learned the hard way; that all of us won't make it. As harsh as a reality as it is, it is one that must be faced. (short pause)... that reminds me of a film that Mrs. Gay showed our class a few weeks back, called "The Days Of Wine and Roses"... (pause) Lesson taught; It's not about how life is treating you, but how you are treating life. It is essential to always remember that we are the masters of our destiny. Even in our weakest and most abandoned state. Stuck in the realm of our lower self and degradation, we sometimes make foolish decisions, and misgovern our lives. (short pause) Given the time to reflect upon our conditions, and search diligently for what is being created and formed within; due to our misgoverning ourselves, we then reach a plateau of where we rise from the ashes, spread our wings, and soar like the Pheonix; dwelling in the epitome of higher thinking. (short pause)... Only by much searching can a miner discover diamonds and gold. So is it with the mind. Man can only find his true self by digging deep into his soul. Understanding this, he begins to realize that he is the molder of life, conqueror of dreams, and ruler over all of his circumstances. (pause)

I say these things to say that, although at one point and time these men may have fallen short of society's expectations, they now make a conscious decision to go right, where as, at one point and time they would have undoubtedly gone left. Looking at myself through each of my counterparts, it would be a travesty if I didn't take this time to commend their efforts and wish them all the best, as they move forward to the next phase and embark on a world-wide mission, into the field of counseling. (pause) (Thank Men)

In part, I want to leave you with this; In more ways than any of you may be able to imagine, this program has helped a lot of men look forward to a brighter future. Where they may have once been undecided about what they were going to do upon their release from prison, they are now equipped with a skill that will help them contribute to making their communities a better place to live in, provide for their families, and show those who had once looked down upon their short comings that they have in fact taken control of their lives, and refused to settle for anything less than what they are worthy of. (pause)...

It was once said that the greatest charity is the gift of education; realizing this, the class of 2010 CASAC graduates once again thanks you for all of your time, dedication and relentless support.

We Thank You!...

If These Prison Walls Could Talk, they would tell the tales of many lies untold. They would reveal explicit details of illicit behavior that unfolds behind closed doors.

They would speak of grown men crying when the lights are turned off at night. They would whisper the prayer of convicts, who pour out their hearts when no one is in sight.

They would expose the atrocities that staff members commit against prisoners. They would pay tribute to those who've overcome the torment and trauma, agony of oppression, suppression, beatings, bruises and blisters.

They would renounce the secrecy of rapes, embrace the cleansing confessions, encourage education, and comfort those who are weary from depression.

They would help hide the plans of those who at night dream of escape. They would also mention the horrible violent clashes, resulting in murder, maiming, decapitation, paralysis and deep lacerations.

They would repeat the songs of inspiring entertainers, encourage prospective book writers, analyze arguments made by legal beagles, and invigorate the romantic exploits of prolific letter writers.

If These Prison Walls Could Talk, they would preach the need for reform, cast aside those who insist on holding on to past detestable ways, and campaign for the many inmates who strive each day for a better and brighter future.

William Bradley

Rochester, New York

The prison population, both state and federal has been steadily increasing since the mid 1980's, despite changes in policies, laws, guidelines, presidential pardons, clemency, and criminal justice reform. This is partly because of the length of sentences that are being given to low level crimes, the lack of funding for treatment programs, and the absence of effective mentoring programs. If this continues, what type of future will the next generation have?...

Chapter Five
"The Future"

We are now entering E-Block.......

Men and women who have excelled in a particular area in life are often times no more gifted than anyone else. But they have been able to do so only because they have taken time out to prepare themselves to develop whatever potential they truly possess. They make a conscious choice to strive in a direction that will better the lives of all of those who come into contact with them and who are willing to learn.

People often reflect without, what they are thinking within. Your quality of life will always be a reflection of your thoughts. Each decision you make will either improve or worsen your conditions. We live in a world of orderly structure. Nothing happens by accident. For your every decision there is a reward; shall it bring about joy or pain. Just as the first domino begins to fall and cause a chain reaction, so your decisions from the past effects your future.

Lest we continue to fall, let us be wise in our decision making. Let us use our past mistakes as a reflection, take full advantage of the present moment and begin our construction in obtaining a prosperous tomorrow. Allow no wall or fence to hinder your progress. Though you may be imprisoned in the physical form, never allow your mind to be locked away.

>>

More Needs To Be Done

More needs to be done when addressing disproportionate minority contact with the judicial system. Communities of color all across the country continue to be utterly over represented in county jails, state prisons and federal institutions; as the multitude of systematic reasons for this dumb-founding disparity has not been properly addressed. The mountainous increase of Blacks and Hispanics in prison must be examined by the public in order for them to see the injustice in racial profiling. We must find a solution if there is any hope of the urban communities ever regaining their bearings.

There has been extensive research done that supports the effectiveness of community based programs. Not only do they increase public safety and give reentrants a more comfortable setting in which to further their rehabilitation, but they also save the tax payers money.

As a credentialed alcohol and substance abuse counselor, mentor and life coach, I am committed to helping anyone who is willing to help themselves. Having lived life on both sides of the fence, I've studied human behavior for nearly two decades, dedicated myself to the betterment of society and feel that there is no one more adequate than a person such as myself to educate those who are in pursuit of a better way of living.

Research has also identified several different strategies that if applied correctly will make significant down turns in our country's recidivism rate. Cognitive behavioral therapy, which helps maladaptive behavior, by changing a persons' irrational thoughts, beliefs and ideas, I feel are one of, if not the main key(s) to solving our problem of over-incarceration................

Proceeding years of long and vigorous studies of myself and learning why I had taken on certain immoral traits in the past, I began to wonder why other men had also decided to turn to a life of crime. In search of the answer to my question, I took on the task of finding individuals who I felt were capable of assisting me in my investigation. Although none of them could be considered candidates for state office, they all met my qualifications; which were honesty, sincerity and showing a willingness to change. In most cases, those are a rarity in prison.

After making my selections, I began to conduct several interviews. Join me in my first one.

Dr. Kevin E. Dolphin: Good morning, sir.

Inmate: Good morning to you, too.

Dr. Kevin E. Dolphin: Before we begin, I want to thank you for your assistance.

Inmate: That's quite alright. You are a good fella; and I believe that if there was ever anything that I could do the help you, I would.

Dr. Kevin E. Dolphin: Would you please state your name for our readers?

Inmate: They all call me Mr. Pratt.

Dr. Kevin E. Dolphin: Where are you from?

Inmate: I'm from Candor, North Carolina..

Dr. Kevin E. Dolphin: Is your mother still alive?

Inmate: Yes.

Dr. Kevin E. Dolphin: If you could say one thing to her at this exact moment, what would it be?

Inmate: I would thank her for seeing no wrong in me. Still to this day, in her eyes, she still loves me.

Dr. Kevin E. Dolphin: How old are you?

Inmate: I'm forty-six.

Dr. Kevin e. Dolphin: What are you in prison for?

Inmate: I'm locked up for conspiracy.

Dr. Kevin E. Dolphin: Conspiracy to do what?

Inmate: Conspiracy to sell fifty kilos, which I had nothing to do with. Many of the people on my indictment, that they call my co-defendants, I ain't never seen befo'!

Dr. Kevin E. Dolphin: How do you feel about the judicial system?

Inmate: I feel that it's messed up! How you gonna' snatch a man off the street, give him some charges that he don't even own, tell him that if he don't snitch, he gonna' get life in prison, convict him in a kangaroo court, and then send him a million miles away from his family!? Now, I'm not sayin' that I'm no saint, but I know I ain't done what they accused me of! This whole thang just makes me bitter! I try not to let it affect me, but it's hard! How can a man come in at twenty and leave at sixty!? That's just horrible! Down right horrible! The system is a warehouse! How can a man have sex wit' a three year old, and get one or two years and another man get fifty years fo' sellin' a twenty dollar rock?! What kinda' justice is that?! I tell ya', it ain't justice! It's injustice all the way 'round the board!

Dr. Kevin E. Dolphin: Who was your biggest influence when you were growing up?

Inmate: A white man named David Kinney. He ran a program call, "Nypum". It stands fo' National Youth Program. It helped kids. I was one of the first kids in the program. It was an experimental program. When I left, ten years ago, he was still runnin' it. He started the program when I was thirteen. He used to come around and pick us up in his own vehicle.

Dr. Kevin E. Dolphin: How did he effect your life?

Inmate: He showed me that all caucasions ain't bad! He was doin' what he was don' to help us. Not fo' no money. He showed me a lot of thangs that helped me get by.

Dr. Kevin E. Dolphin: How did you get caught up in the streets?

Inmate: I would say bad choices! And feelin' that by doin' certain thangs, I was takin' care of my family. Boy, was I wrong! Never could I see anything like this comin'! These folks done damnear took my whole life away, fo' somethin' I know I ain't did!

Dr. Kevin E. Dolphin: If there was one thing in life that you could do over, what would it be?

Inmate: I would never love nothin' more than I love myself. Because the love of somethin' more than you love yourself cause you to make some bad choices. Such as the kind that could cause you to spend life in prison, behind these walls! When I look back, I can honestly say that I loved money more than I loved myself. Money put a lot of eye patches on us, covered our eyes and lead us to these type of situations.

Dr. Kevin E. Dolphin: Again, I want to thank you for your help, Mr. Pratt.

Inmate: No. Thank you.

During the time that I had been conducting the series of interviews, my counselor, Mrs. Diehl approached me about assisting her with coming up with some sort of therapeutic program that would help the inmates find some sort of way to do their time more productively. Ray Brook was a very tense place. Not only was it a medium max, where most violent offenders, gang members, and lifers were sent for various reasons, but it was also one of the most tyrannical prisons on the east coast. **If These Prison Walls Could Talk**; they would give graphic details of all of the senseless assaults that take place there, almost each day.

Having already been putting together some sort of program of my own when Mrs. Diehl called me to her office, we sat down and came up with a mens' discussion group, called **"Back To The Future"**. Since I had been an inmate at the institution for over eight years, carried myself in a reputable manner and was well known by everyone, she felt that I would have a huge influence in making the program a success; and so it was. So many people had signed up for the class that we had to do a back log that carried well into the next year.

Back To the Future

A reflection of your past, an in depth look at your present situation, and an application of successful cognitive development tools to assist you in living a productive life in the future.

Group Outline

This group will be offered twice a year. In January and July. It will meet for two hours, for twelve weeks, on the correctional counselors scheduled late night to discuss and share with other participants various issues, experiences and changes that has taken place in ones' life. It will encourage ways for individuals to realize what mistakes have been made in their past and the effects such decision making has had in their lives and the lives of their families. It will allow them to see what they could have done differently and how they will make choices in the future. Topics will be discussed in an open forum, among all participants.

Discussions will consist of the following:

- **Past life experiences**
- **Trauma**
- **Recognizing mistakes and their impact**
- **Fatherhood**
- **Anger Management**
- **Employment**
- **Education/Financial Literacy**
- **Substance abuse, Conflict Resolution and Decision Making.......**

❖ **Group members will be encouraged to discuss and share ways to do their incarcerated time in a productive manner; enabling them to set goals, improve their social skills, understand culture diversity and strengthen their family relations.**

As I stood in front of twenty-six inmates, who were eager to participate in what would be another historical moment at FCI Ray Brook, I reminded them of how important that it was for them to give all that they could, and in return, they would receive a strong sense of accomplishment and relief. The information provided would open up new portals in their minds, give them a new sense of living and change their lives.

"This class is to help give us all a deep insight into the lives we live. Past and present. My reason for forming this forum with Mrs. Diehl is to hopefully provide someone with a new perspective on the way that life and the conditions that surround it are viewed. More times than not, I look around at the individuals who are in the same position that I am in and shake my head. You ask why? Because their conduct of ill-mannered, irresponsibility and lack of respect for themselves and others leaves me to wonder about the future of their children! This saddens me more than any of you may be able to realize. –Understanding the need for change, I know that if we don't re-align our perspectives, most of our children will be representatives in places like this. When you change your beliefs, you change your expectations. When you change your attitude, you change your behavior. When you change your behavior, you change your performance. When you change your performance, you change your life. –Ultimately, you get out of life exactly what you put into it"…

I went on to have each member of the group introduce themselves. In doing so, I felt that it would draw us closer together and create a more comfortable setting. During our first two hour session, we discussed everything from daily self-reflections to who our role models were when we were growing up. In between topics, I would have Mrs. Diehl interject her point of view. I felt that having someone else who lived a totally different lifestyle give an assessment on what was being said often times gave the inmates more meat to chew on. Aside from them learning from her rationalization, she also got an understanding of who they were, and why they thought the way that they did. In that way, I felt that she would be better equipped to meet their needs as a staff member and as a counselor.

-Delighted by how much I thought that we had accomplished during our meeting, I stood before the inmates again, at the end of the session.

"The garment that we knit today, should be one that will protect us from the storm of regret and despair when one fails to take advantage of his/her opportunities and invest in life. –Understand that your entire existence here on earth should be looked at as an investment. Wherever you find great investment, you will find great return. Life doesn't afford us the luxury of paying a small percentage and still receiving a huge gain. We must invest today if we are to reap the rewards of tomorrow! Your insight into the future is a reflection of your past. How much are you willing to invest in yourself? For those of you who are ready to return home to a state of consciousness, and direct your thoughts to a higher plane, I ask that you continue on this journey with me…..As we bring this first group discussion to a close, I hope that something we touched on has given someone a different retrospect about some of the past events in their life. –I also ask that you contemplate on these issues and choose your future course more wisely. –Thank you for coming. See you next week."

*For two and a half months, the **Back To The Future** mens' discussion group went on with all of its participants looking forward to the next meeting. Although a couple of inmates may have missed a class here and there, no one dropped out.*

*Understanding the need for such a therapeutic program inside of these turbulent and unstable environments, I hope to one day play a part in establishing **Back To the Future** discussion groups in county jails, state prisons and federal institutions all across the United States.*

Educate/Incarcerate

Statistics have shown that inmates who acquire some sort of education while incarcerated are less likely to return to prison after their release....

Today, more than ever before, being locked behind bars seems like common life to uneducated minorities. Those who have dropped out of school are expected to be dead or in state or federal prison within several years of their withdrawal. This ongoing occurrence, which has increased over the last thirty years has unconsciously created an under-class of social outsiders who have become foreigners to the rest of society. They are aliens in their own country. Despite having been born right here the in the U.S.

Along with a lack of education, the so called **WAR ON DRUGS** has nearly crippled Black and Hispanic communities. What is allowing to be done undermines the principles that the justice system claims that America stands for. The land of equal opportunity is for some, a place of inequality and injustice.

A combination of a criminal record and no education will most likely lead back to a life of crime and indecency. Knowledge is truly power! Education is critical on all levels of our existence. It creates leaders of all kinds; in government, the industrial systems, corporate sectors and in our communities. The lack there of mires us with an uncontrollable problem in the future.

According to the U.S. Department of Education for every dollar that is spent on prison college educational programs, the tax payers save two dollars. With the expel of Pell College Grants in 1994, for those prisoners who had a desire to learn, it made it increasingly difficult for them to be able to rise above their challenges.

Statistics – According to Pew, in collaboration with the association of State correction Administration (ASCA), 4 out of 10 adults reoffend within three years of release.

As sad and stark as this reality may be, it is one that must be faced and met head on with an unrelenting determination to overcome. Without such an attitude, the weight of incarceration will continue to crush education. We must persist in our learning at all cost; for in doing so, we remain competitive, competent and productive.

"It was once said that the gift of knowledge is the greatest charity of all but there are times when it will only be given to those who refuse to give up their pursuit to acquire it"...

Your Future

You alone must make the choice to achieve your success; and in doing so, maintain control of your future. Nothing should ever be taken for granted. There are no guarantees in life. You are bound to encounter storms, negative forces, injustices and natural disasters on your journey. Your personal power of choice can put you in position to handle and overcome any obstacle that may arise. Possession of this power gives you the strength to be able to navigate through difficult situations and remain positive when everyone else around you has unmanned their sense of direction.

Understanding how consequential certain choices are when it comes to your future, you will not bother troubling your mind with worse possibility type scenarios. You become aware that circumstances often become magnified by the way you view them, and that what you decide to do with those thoughts will lead to an end result....Failure or Success...

To put it bluntly, you will become what you choose to become. Let failure be discarded and championed by the man/woman who has found purpose. The crown of victory is only worn by those who dare to make the correct choices, leave negativity behind and find themselves ascending on the door step of success..........

The O.G. Wise Man

If These Prison Walls Could Talk

For some time now, it has been suggested that community corrections; such as intervention and day treatment programs be used rather than prison for non-violent offenders. In doing so, it could help reverse the recidivism rate, give minorities a better chance at being successful in an ever-growing job market and help avert billions of dollars in prison costs. From my studies, I have yet to see the government take this into serious consideration and act on it.

Public Safety

*"It's time to end business as usual in our prison system and for legislators to think and act with courage and creativity. We can make sensible and proven reforms to our criminal justice system that will cut costs, while keeping the public safe". –****Newt Gingrich**** ® Former House Speaker; January 8, 2011***

Decades of research have produced ample evidence and professional consensus about which case management strategies most effectively reduce recidivism and improve public safety. Effective community supervision begins with validated risk and needs assessment, and the accurate categorization of offenders by their risk of re-offending.

The identification of risk and needs is a critical step, because supervision and programs are most effective at reducing future crime when they are geared towards focusing on an offenders individual profile. Failing to match treatment with an offenders risk level can have serious consequences.

At least 95% of inmates in America will at some point be released and turned back to the communities from which they left. Keeping them crime and drug-free is no easy task. Many offenders lacked education, work experience, family support and stable living situations before they were incarcerated. Many others suffer from mental illness or a history of addiction.

What is to be done to help these ex-offenders and increase public safety? Locking them back up definitely isn't the answer. In my opinion, counseling, mentoring, educational programs, job skill programs, social programs and other intervention programs would help. When you assist in changing a persons thought pattern, you help change their behavior.

"Prisons are often the forgotten element of the criminal justice system, until things go badly. Catching the guy and prosecuting him is really important work, but if we don't do anything with that individual after we've got him, then shame on us. If all that effort goes to waste, and we just open the doors five years later, and it's the same guy reentering back into society, with the same criminal thinking, we've failed in our mission". **Minnesota Commissioner of Corrections, Tom Roy. April 7, 2001**

As we tour the far wing of the Block, we are met by an inmate who has just completed a seventeen year prison sentence, and this is what he had to say:

Gary Raheem Watkins

AKA

Suliaman

If These Prison Walls Could Talk......What Would They Say?..

"When the topic of discussion comes to mind, one has to ponder on the many variations of incarceration. Never will physical or mental bondage be able to consume the man who declares himself free! Rehabilitation hasn't shown its face inside here in over thirty-somethin' years!

Penitentiary-Relating to incurring confinement

Penitence-Remorse; regret for sin or wrong doing

Repentance-Sad and humble realization of and regret for ones misdeeds....

Penitentiary derives from the word **Penitence**. To repent adds the implication of a resolve to change by a complete change of character. Some inhabitants inside of these places become complacent with their situations, accept the circumstances behind it and lie dormant.

The prison walls cry to be left alone. The first man trapped inside of the cell tells the second man; Listen young buck! You're violatin' my air space! You need to know that I wouldn't share my hell with another; for the burden is beyond the weight that anyone should carry!

It is utterly trifling to find a human being living content inside of anyone of these dark holes! Man finds peace or peace of mind in solitude; yet, that's only because he is unable to escape it.

Trapped in the Twilight Zone, caught hanging out inside the Sci-Fi channel ain't even on the same page as what really goes on behind these walls. Speaking from age old experience up close and personal. Ain't nothin' good about this place! If you could see half of the foolery I see, on a day to day basis, you would most likely pray for blindness. Knowing what I know now, in all honesty, I wish that all men would leave this place and never, ever return!

Hearing the screams, witnessing the nonstop flow of tears. The deafening mourns at night. The rapes, the robberies, the suicides and the murders!

Control through treatment. Treatment through control. Chaos and confusion to keep control. Subliminal seduction; the control over the human mind.

Inmate! Convict! Prisoner!... Several different mentalities. Trauma of thought within.

Monsters are created behind these walls! The inhabitants can either flourish or become stagnant.

Many young souls grow old inside of these decrepit places. Manhood is often lost and found here. The weak become strong. The strong become weak. The sane lose their sanity. The naive get preyed upon. The violent rule the kingdom unknown to society.

How many judges, lawyers and crooked district attorneys are to blame for this debacle?! I witness lifes' everyday dilemma of a man who has been cast into the lions den. In such a crazy place, ones own balance is to act crazy.

Behind these walls, sinners become saints. Saints become mongrels. The fool is made wise. The wise seek for answers to roads previously travelled. A mans mind becomes tarnished from dwelling too long in the wilderness. Our main logic may be another mans madness.

If These Prison Walls Could Talk, they'd scream for liberty, promote equality, ban racial injustice and inform society of what really goes on inside of these institutions....

Three Strikes

Did you know that due to the "Three Strikes" law, a huge number of Blacks and Hispanics are likely to spend life in prison. Because of the disproportion of racial injustice that is more likely to affect minorities than whites, the U.S. will continue to mount staggering cost to house inmates who in many cases should have been deferred to a treatment program.

The Company You Keep

It is better to be alone than in the wrong company....Tell me who your best friends are and I will tell you who you are. If you run with wolves, you will learn how to howl. But if you associate with eagles, you will learn how to soar to great heights. *"A mirror reflects a mans face, but who he truly is will be shown by the kind of friends he chooses"*. The simple but true fact of life is that you become like those with whom you closely associate. –For the good or the bad!

The less you associate with some people, the more your life will improve. Anytime you tolerate mediocrity in others, it increases you mediocrity. An important attribute in successful people is their impatience with negative thinking and negative acting people. As you grow, your associates will change. Some of your friends will want you to stay where they are. Friends that don't help you climb will want you to crawl. Your friends will stretch your vision or choke your dream. Those that don't increase you will eventually decrease you....

Consider this; never receive counsel from unproductive people. Never discuss your problems with someone incapable of contributing to the solution. Because those who never succeed themselves are always the first to tell you how. Not everyone has a right to speak into your life. You are certain to get the worst of the bargain when you exchange ideas with the wrong person.

Spend Your Time Wisely

The strength of character gained through lifes' trials will be the true measure of a mans' success. In our existence, whether it be behind prison walls or out in society, we should conceive a legitimate purpose, set out to accomplish it with our whole being and devote ourselves to its attainment. Using time as our ally, we must always be aware of how we spend it. Spending your time foolishly will never amount to anything. Spending your time wisely will afford you the advantage to see through many of the illusions that once blinded you in the past...

-The future is now, what are you going to do with it? The walls may remain standing, the chainz of imprisonment may never be loosened and the echoes of injustice may continue to sing its song, but never do you have to allow them to thwart your evolution and advancement....

Chapter Six
The Message

Be mindful of the wet floor sign, as we enter F-Block…

U.S. Incarceration Rate

Black Males: **4,347 per 100,000**

Latino Males: **1,755 per 100,000**

White Males: **678 per 100,000**

2010 Bureau Of Justice Statistics

As you compare the staggering numbers between males in the **U.S. Incaration Rate**, it is evident that something is definitely wrong with our justice system. Although I will admit that law makers seem to turn a blind eye at times, I must also admit that they are not fully at fault. For those of us who understand that prevention is better than the cure, it is our responsibility to educate those who have yet to extricate themselves from the entanglement of partisanship. So many leaders from the past has sacrificed their well being in order for us to be able to live a life of equality. They did not do so for us to become identified by institutional numbers, and treated as if we are unfit to congregate with the law abiding, upstanding citizens of society. Cages were created for animals; meaning something that is wild and needs to be tamed. When placed behind a prison wall that is exactly how we are viewed by others. Whether we find ourselves in a situation by design or by our own free-will of choice, we have the power to realign our footing and change our entire state of affairs….

Aware of how grave it is for us to renew our minds, I constantly reflect back on the historical letter that was written by Dr. Martin Luther King, Jr., from a Birmingham jail cell. His words were so powerfully written that they touched the very core of my soul. They called me to accountability.

In his missive, he talked about being in Birmingham, because injustice was there; and how he had a job to do. He was unable to sit idly in Atlanta and act as if the mangled state of his fellow kinsmen didn't trouble him. He wrote about how injustice anywhere was a threat to justice everywhere. He understood that all men are caught in an inescapable network of mutuality, which is tied to a single garment of destiny. Whatever effects one, directly effects all, indirectly.

Dr. Martin Luther King Jr.'s sacrifices, like so many others who stood at the forefront of the battlefield with him were immeasurable. If he were still alive today, he would be proud of how far his dream has come; but on the other hand, he would be saddened by the tremendous weight that the United States judicial system has placed on the backs of minorities. He would urge us to stand up. His time in that darkened Birmingham jail cell wasn't spent there so that you and I could end up in one….

Join me in my second interview, inside F-Blocks Quiet Room

June 23, 2010

Dr. Kevin E. Dolphin: Good Afternoon.

Inmate: Good Afternoon to you, too. Thank you for having me.

Dr. Kevin E. Dolphin: The pleasure is mines. For our readers, could you state your name?

Inmate: Mr. Louis 'Canali' Reed, Esquire.

Dr. Kevin E. Dolphin: Where are you from?

Inmate: Bridgeport, Connecticut.

Dr. Kevin E. Dolphin: Is your mother still alive?

Inmate: Yes.

Dr. Kevin E. Dolphin: If there was one thing that you could say to her at this very moment, what would it be?

Inmate: I would tell her that she never has to spend another night worrying about me, because the greatest gift that I have given myself, which in turn I have given her is my relationship with Christ.

Dr. Kevin E. Dolphin: Do you have children?

Inmate: Yes.

Dr. Kevin E. Dolphin: If you could say one thing to your children, what would it be?

Inmate: I want to be to them all that I wanted my parents to be to me.

Dr. Kevin E. Dolphin: How do you feel about the judicial system?

Inmate: If I had to summarize it up in four words, without being bias, it would be black robes, white justice.

Dr. Kevin E. Dolphin: Why those terms?

Inmate: Because I feel that our judicial system is used much more for a racial prophylactic than the equal administration of justice.

Dr. Kevin E. Dolphin: Do you feel that people on the outside are doing enough to help inmates?

Inmate: I feel that the inmates on the inside aren't doing enough to help themselves! It shouldn't take women, particularly to be the vanguard of judicial rights! Especially when men make up the majority of those who are incarcerated in this country! So, if the men who are locked up went home and got involved with campaigns for judicial equality, the results of mass incarceration would tumble. The help would be coming from inside-out! But to answer your question, No! I don't think inmates get enough help from the outside.

Dr. Kevin E. Dolphin: Do you think that fathers not being there for their children leads towards their one day ending up in prison?

Inmate: For my senior report, for my degree towards my Bachelors in Psychology; which was entitled **"That's Just My Babys' Daddy"**, - Fatherlessness, and its impact on people of color; I discovered that eighty-five percent of incarcerated prisoners were fatherless. Sixty-eight percent of black children are born without a father, yet a hundred percent of those children were conceived by a father. So if you look at the raw statistical terms, there is a direct correlation between fatherlessness and incarceration.

Dr. Kevin E. Dolphin: Thank you for your time, Mr. Reed.

Inmate: Again, thank you for having me.

U.S. Incarceration Rate

The Scale Of Disparity

Racial disparities in incarceration can arise from a variety of circumstances. These might include a high rate of minority incarceration, low rate of white incarceration, or varying combinations.

Bureau Of Justice Statistics 2016

-Incarceration is not equal opportunity punishment.

If These Prison Walls Could Talk...What Would They Say?

If These Prison Walls Could Talk, would they defend the rights of those whose voices that have been silenced by the implication of a chronicle of unwarranted laws?

Would they scream foul play?

Would they ask for a recount of the ballots, and urge the minorities to show up at the polls and cast their votes?

If These Prison Walls Could Talk, would they give a eulogy for all of those who have been sentenced to life behind bars, without the possibility of parole?

Would they campaign for more intervention, re-entry, educational, drug treatment programs, and reform?

Would they stand at the doors of the law libraries and invite everyone in, or would they give up hope, throw away all of the books, shut down the computers and allow injustice to continue?

If These Prison Walls Could Talk, what would they actually say?

An Officer and An Inmate

During the time that I was conducting the interviews with various inmates, I also managed to convince three correctional officers to give me a few minutes of their time. It was a known fact that they were trained to think that all prisoners were liers, manipulative, dangerous and untrustworthy. Having observed and studied their behaviors for the past several years, I wanted to know firsthand a little more about their ideologies. Some of what I found was very surprising.

In agreement to participate in this project, all of the officers stipulated that their names could not be used. I had no objections.

August 7, 2010

Dr. Kevin E. Dolphin: How do you feel about inmates?

Officer #1: I don't look at inmates as inmates. I look at and deal with inmates as people. That is why the guys have so much respect for me around here. I believe in treating everyone as individuals. You can't deal with everyone as a whole. That is where you will run into problems.

Dr. Kevin E. Dolphin: Do you feel that inmates are treated fairly by the system?

Officer #1: Actually, I don't. I don't feel that there is enough opportunities for you guys to better yourselves, so that you can make it once you get out of here.

Dr. Kevin E. Dolphin: What would you changed about the federal system?

Officer #1: I would change a lot of the programming in the system.

Dr. Kevin E. Dolphin: Give me an example?

Officer #1: For example, some state facilities allow inmates to build furniture, make clothes and sell their art in local stores. That way, they are able to work on a trade and help take care of their families at the same time. They don't do that in the feds.

Dr. Kevin E. Dolphin: Thank you.

August 7, 2010
(Later that morning)

Dr. Kevin E. Dolphin: How do you feel about inmates?

Officer #2: I feel that inmates are the lowest life form! They are cons and are always looking for a short cut in life. They commit crimes and expect for the taxpayers to take care of them. They are irresponsible, ignorant and a disgrace to the entire human race!

Dr. Kevin E. Dolphin: Do you feel that inmates are treated fairly?

Officer #2: Fairly?! I feel that you guys aren't punished enough! The prison system is too soft, if you ask me! The punishment is not severe enough! If I had my way, all inmates would live off bread and water. You would also have to work for free. There would be no television or recreation! You would work and be locked inside of your cells.

Dr. Kevin E. Dolphin: That's kind of harsh, don't you think?

Officer #2: (laughs) It isn't harsh enough!

Dr. Kevin E. Dolphin: If you could, what would you change about the federal system?

Officer #2: If I could change things, I would cut family visits and bring back capital punishment! I would cut all programs! I don't want you guys becoming smarter criminals! I want you punished for the crimes you committed!

Dr. Kevin E. Dolphin: Thank you.

August 7, 2010
(That same evening)

Dr. Kevin E. Dolphin: How do you feel about inmates?

Officer #3: I feel that a lot of inmates just make a lot of bad decisions in their lives. Whether it be from circumstances or out of following the wrong crowd. I feel that most of them deserve another chance. Everyone doesn't learn at the same rate of speed. Some of us learn after our second mistake. Some of us never learn. For the most part, I judge people by how they carry themselves. I do my best not to stereo type any of you guys. That isn't fair or professional.

Dr. Kevin E. Dolphin: Do you feel that inmates are treated fairly?

Officer #3: I feel that the system has its pros and its cons! I'm just gonna' leave it at that.

Dr. Kevin E. Dolphin: What would you change about the federal system?

Officer #3: I would bring back federal parole. I would also encourage family members to be more supportive to you guys. I feel that we need more programs. Mainly drug and alcohol and anger management. There is also a huge need for more education! Without schooling, these places will continue to stay over crowded! Every time we let one go, there is three waiting to fill that empty bed! We need new laws and we need to shut some of the prisons down! It's just down right ridiculous.

Dr. Kevin E. Dolphin: Thank you

Research records show at times the unemployment rate for ex-felons reaches as high as 50%. In some cases, it is extremely difficult for someone with a criminal history to find employment after their incarceration. Many employers just flat out refuse to hire them. Although some states have done away with criminal back ground checks, there are those who continue to use it as a form of discrimination.

Join me in another interview as we come into the F-Block common area…

Dr. Kevin E. Dolphin: Good afternoon, sir.

Inmate: What's up, homeboy.

Dr. Kevin E. Dolphin: For the readers, can you state your name?

Inmate: Just call me A.D.

Dr. Kevin E. Dolphin: Ok, A.D. Where are you from?

Inmate: Boston, Massachusetts.

Dr. Kevin E. Dolphin: How long have you been locked up?

Inmate: I been down for five years.

Dr. Kevin E. Dolphin: How has your being incarceration effected your family?

Inmate: It has effected them tremendously. I was snatched away from them without a warning.

Dr. Kevin E. Dolphin: Do you have children?

Inmate: Yes.

Dr. Kevin E. Dolphin: How many?

Inmate: Seven.

Dr. Kevin E. Dolphin: If you could say one thing to your children, what would it be?

Inmate: I would tell them to live life to the fullest, but while living your life to do something positive and constructive. Not to waste time.

Dr. Kevin E. Dolphin: As an older gentlemen, who is often referred to as an O.G. around here, how do you feel about the youth?

Inmate: At times, I feel as though generation x is a lost cause. Simply because they won't accept guidance. But I have to remember that I was once their age, and how the elders used to reach out to me. You can only pass down knowledge to those who are willing to listen.

Dr. Kevin E. Dolphin: Do you feel that inmates receive the support that they should get from the outside?

Inmate: Absolutely not!

Dr. Kevin E. Dolphin: Why do you feel that way?

Inmate: Society has turned their backs on those who are incarcerated. Our ancestors fought and died for the struggle! Whether it was out in society or behind these walls! I feel that much, much more can be done on our behalf! I look at it as people turning their backs, because they don't want to fight! Whether right or wrong; the man or woman behind bars is being victimized! Back in the day, the struggle was for justice! There is so much injustice that has taken place throughout history in this country that the entire court system should be brought up on charges!

Dr. Kevin E. Dolphin: Thank you for your time, A.D.

Inmate: The struggle goes on.

The Message

In many ways, the past, the present and the future are chained together in unbreakable links. Throughout our journey, we will be presented with an onslaught of messages. Some will be to our benefit, while others, our detriment. Understand that where there is harmony, conflict lives in the cell next door. Whether granted equality or down trodden in injustice, fight a good fight, and never, ever turn your backs on those who remain in the struggle.

Chapter Seven
Lessons Learned

Considered by correctional staff to be the worst unit in the prison, G-Block houses many of the inmates who refuse to learn from life lessons. A Host of these individuals, including myself are repeat offenders and have been handed lengthy sentences by the courts. Why does such a destructive behavior continue, and where does it derive from?

-Albert Bandura suspected that aggressive behavior, in particular, is subject to OBSERVATIONAL LEARNING and that aggression and violence on television programs, including cartoons, tend to increase aggression in children. (Violence portrayed on television as an acceptable way to solve problems often encourages aggressive behavior in children).

When a certain way of thinking or doing something is implanted in the mind at a young age, it tends to fashion and shape the character of the individual as they grow older. Movies, television and music are perfect examples of this.

Banduras research provided the impetus for studying the effects of televised violence and aggression in both cartoons and regular programming. Despite the awareness of society acknowledging the negative impact of social media, some movies, television programs and music, the violence portrayed is still excessive. The problem is compounded by the fact that the average family watches more than seven hours of television, and is constantly distracted by nonessential issues on the internet each day. Watching excessive violence and listening to vulgar depictions in music gives people an exaggerated view of the pervasiveness of violence in society, while making them less sensitive to the victims who are perpetrated upon. The same thing can also be said about drug use and other forms of crime.

What can be done to correct this behavior once it has become a strong part of an individual's psychological makeup?

-According to B.F. Skinner, punishment does not extinguish an undesirable behavior; rather it suppresses that behavior when the punishing agent is present. But the behavior is apt to continue when the threat of punishment is unlikely. If punishment (imprisonment, fines and so on) reliably extinguished unlawful behavior, there would be fewer repeat offenders in the criminal justice system.

Punishment indicates that a certain behavior is unacceptable, but does not help people develop more appropriate behaviors. If punishment is to be used, it should be administered in conjunction with reinforcement or rewards of appropriate behavior.

The person who is severely punished often times becomes fearful and feel angry and hostile towards the punisher. These reactions may be accompanied by a desire to retaliate or to avoid or escape from the punisher and the punishing situation. Many runaway teens leave home to escape physical abuse. Punishment that involves a loss of privileges is more effective than physical punishment and engenders less fear and hostility. (**Waters & Gusec, 1977**)

Punishment frequently leads to aggression. Those who administer physical punishment may become models of aggressive behavior—people who demonstrate aggression as a way of solving problems and discharging anger. Children of abusive, punishing parents are at greater risk than other children of becoming aggressive and abusive themselves. (**Widom, 1989**)

Many psychologist believe that removing the rewarding consequences of undesirable behavior is the best way to extinguish a problem behavior. Others disagree. What is your view?

The intensity of the punishment should match the seriousness of the misdeed. Unjust, severe punishment is likely to produce more negative behaviors. If the behavior is to be suppressed, the punishment must be more punishing than the misbehavior is rewarding. –A person who wishes to apply punishment must understand that the purpose of punishment is not to vent anger, but to modify undesirable behavior.

Almost two thirds of minority drug arrests result in a criminal conviction…

An estimated 68% of minority convicted felony drug offenders are sentenced to jail or prison…

White Americans were arrested more than any other race for murder in 2008, making up nearly 43% of all arrests. African Americans, constituting approximately 12% of the general population, were significantly over represented in total arrests made. African Americans were also over represented in victimizations, representing 47% of all murder victims. White Americans and individuals of other races were significantly underrepresented in cases of murder and non-negligible homicide in 2008. Murder in white American and African American populations were overwhelming interracial, with 83% of all white victims and 90% of all black victims having been murdered by individuals of the same race. The same was true, though to a lesser degree for individuals of other races, with 52% having been murdered by individuals also of other races. (**This is according to: Wikipedia, The Free Encyclopedia**)

If The Prison Walls Could Talk

If These Prison Walls Could Talk, their voices would paint a picture so vivid that it would separate the strong from the weak.

They would tell the inconsistencies of man, their naughty behaviors; all the way down to their animalistic rituals.

They would never lie, so their words would be pillars of truth that stood on facts. Not fiction. Real...and not fake. Though the secrets that were meant to be hidden would be boxed in the corner of the light. –Light is truth; darkness is falsehood. So when the lights are out, "THEY", the four corners of the earth will see all things...

Don't get it confused, these walls can smell the fear and hear the tears before they fall.

They can turn some to men or make cowards of all.

If These Prison Walls Could Talk, they would remind you to always remain conscious of your words and actions. Life presents many enlightening lessons for those who are willing to learn.

K. Simmons-EL

"The Moore"

Lost Tears

During the time of my incarceration, I had the privilege of meeting many different individuals, who all came from various walks of life. Some of them I was able to learn from, while others had nothing to offer, except a seat, where they sat at the table of ignorance, and dined in simple ineptness.

Read and learn while I share this short non-fiction story with you;

"Yo, Belvadere! What you doin' back?!" I asked the fifty-seven year old African American male from Trenton, New Jersey. He had only been out on the streets for a little over 90 days; after having done twenty-two years in federal prison for bank robbery.

Raising his head, as he entered the front door of the unit, he smiled half- heartedly, "I got caught up in the mix, young buck! You know how it is"

Waiting until he had placed his bed roll down on the table, I continued, "What you mean, you got caught up in the mix? What you back on, a lil' violation?"

"Nah." He mumbled, unable to meet my questioning gaze. "I got a new one."

"A new one?! I frowned.

"Yea, a new one! I got a new case, youngin."

"Man, stop playin'!" I shook my head, just knowing that he was playing.

As if he was trying desperately to find his voice, Belvadere cleared his throat. "I ain't jokin'." He replied. "I got caught up trying ta' help my man, Floss and 'em knock this liquor store off."

"A liquor store?!"

"Yea. These Italian dudes we knew was sittin' on a lot of money, so we decided to run up in the place."

I frowned. "What happened to all that stuff you told me about goin' out there, takin' care of ya' moms?! I guess that went out the window, ha"?"

Belvadere shook his dead. "It's kinda' hard tryin' ta' take care of somebody when you ain't got nothin ya'self!"

"So, now what?" I asked in disappointment.

"I gotta' do seventeen years." He had a somber look on his face.

"Seventeen years?!"

"Yea. That's what I had to plea out to in order to stop from gettin' life."

I stood there for a moment, and thought about all of the talks that I had with Belvadere in the past. I remembered him telling me about how much his mother needed him out there, and how he looked forward to being the type of son that she deserved. At his age, he would probably never see the streets, again. He had spent the majority of his life in and out of prison. And as things stood, this could very well be his final resting place. "If you need anything, come up to my cell later on." I finally said, with a note of sadness in my voice.

"Okay, youngin." He responded before picking up his bed roll and heading towards the c.o.'s office. "As soon as I get situated, I'ma' come up and kick it wit' you."

As I watched Belvadere turn and walk away, all I could think about was his mother and the countless number of other women who had shed lost tears for men like him and I.

Did you know that white Americans were arrested more than any other race for non-lethal violent crimes in 2008; that made up 50% of all arrests.

African Americans were significantly overrepresented for non-lethal crimes in 2008; which made up for 39% of all arrest. (This is according to Race and Crime In the United States. Wikipedia, The free Encyclopedia)

Join me for another interview inside of the prison library:

August 3, 2010

Dr, Kevin E. Dolphin: Good Morning.

Inmate: Good mornin' to you, too.

Dr. Kevin E. Dolphin: Thank you for coming.

Inmate: Thanks for invitin' me.

Dr. Kevin E. Dolphin: For the readers, could you state your name?

Inmate: Just call me, Big Spence.

Dr. Kevin E. Dolphin: Where are you from, Big Spence?

Inmate: I'm from Buffalo, New York.

Dr. Kevin E. Dolphin: How long have you been locked up?

Inmate: I been behind bars this time for approximately twelve years.

Dr. Kevin E. Dolphin: So, you are a repeat offender?

Inmate: Yes

Dr. Kevin E. Dolphin: How many times have you been to prison?

Inmate: This is my third time. First federal bid.

Dr. Kevin E. Dolphin: How has your incarceration this time affected your family?

Inmate: First and foremost, I believe that I was the glue that held everything together. Where I once had a functional family, I now have a dysfunctional one. Being incarcerated has not only deteriorated my family structure, but it has also disrupted the growth process that is essential and necessary for the structure of the community where I live. That being said, I have to look deep inside my own person and understand that a lot of what has transpired over the last twelve years is the manifestation of my own ignorance to make proper decisions. But from indecision has also arisen a man that has been reborn. Behind these walls, I have totally transformed myself from being incomplete to becoming more complete. The way that I've accomplished that is by redirecting that ignorance that once held me hostage; that same ignorance that created the disfunction of my family structure.

Dr. Kevin E. Dolphin: Do you have children?

Inmate: Yes.

Dr. Kevin E. Dolphin: How many?

Inmate: Four boys.

Dr. Kevin E. Dolphin: If you could say one thing to them all, what would it be??

Inmate: It would probably be this... During the course of my forty-nine years on this earth, I've always believed that we couldn't control our circumstances. Although our environment plays a big part in the development of our personalities and influences us in numerous ways, we alone have the power to dictate and control our circumstance. I've heard many people complain about their circumstances and conditions, but never about what they are going to do to change them. We must understand that the mind is capable of anything. The past, the present and how we view the future is in it. Those three elements are essential when it comes to changing your conditions and circumstances. Be the author of your fate. No deposit, no return.

Dr. Kevin E. Dolphin: What is one of the most important things that you've learned during your incarceration?

Inmate: One of the most important things I learned is this... every individual has an assortment of characteristics and personalities. Inside of each person there can be a king, a fool, there can be a gladiator, a nightingale, an athlete, an intellectual and so on. Now, the thing is this; during the course of this time, I've discovered the most important thing is that you have to capture and cultivate the individual that you were created to be. Because, if you don't you will continue to go through life with a diversity of character defects. You will never hone in on your true craft. When you are unable to figure out who you truly are, there will be all types of chaotic situations surrounding your existence. Never will you find peace, or find that ability to break free of old habits.

Dr. Kevin E. Dolphin: If there was something that you could say to your community, what would it be?

Inmate: The first thing I would do is make amends by apologizing for my boyish acts. I would apologize for failing to apply myself in the needed and necessary way to enrich those who live around me; from young to old. I now see and understand that ignorance is a liability. To be ignorant of your ignorance is stupidity! Many people promise more than they are able. They promise the perfection of ten, and discharge less than a tenth of a percent of one. Having aquired that knowledge, I won't make any promises, but I will make a pledge; that upon my release, I will put my best foot forward. To bring about clarity and the much needed understanding about the dangers of not finishing school, not respecting your parents, participating in drugs, disrespecting women, and not knowing and realizing the true power and potential that we hold as a people.

Dr. Kevin E. Dolphin: Thank you for sharing your time.

Inmate: No problem at all.

Did you know that in the late 80's and 90's into the 2000's, with the explosion in the federal prison population, at the height of the governments "WAR ON DRUGS," SOME PRISONS WERE OPERATING AT 150% CAPACITY! Single cells were turned into doubles, then came four men and six men cells. Most T.V. rooms were converted into twelve man cells, with only one toilet. In many institutions these insensate conditions still exist, today.

Work To Be Done

Returning from my early morning work-out, I found this letter sitting on the desk, inside of my cell.

Mr. Dolphin,

It has been my pleasure to meet and greet you. In my eyes, you are the epitome of what we should be doing while enduring this trying time in our lives. I never really got a chance to tell you my story; but in many ways, we come from the same background. Keep doing what you do, because you are effective with young people. I had lost the faith that I once had in our youth, until I witnessed you going hard to convince a young dude that he needs to come up with a more viable plan than drug dealing. Just like Barack Obama will serve as our restoring sun to greatness, we must be Prodigal sons, returning home. Will it be all feasts and celebrations, or will we get busy taking our rightful places at the table of life? We certainly are the heads of our families and communities. They need us more than we ever realized.

*We have much work to do! Failure is not an option. Na'im Akbar describes the male, the boy, and **THE MAN**. We know too much to continue to conduct ourselves as boys. As I leave you with a verse from the Bible and Sura 55 from the Quran, be encouraged that I, among many others are rooting for your success.*

Peace

& Love

"Buddah"

Edward Watts #13013-053

Sura 55: 1-5   **All praise due to Allah. The most merciful, who taught man the Quaran, and taught him eloquent speech…**

1st Corinthians 13:11 *When I was a child, I spoke and though as a child. But, when I became a man, I put aside all childish things…*

If These Prison Walls Could Talk

If These Prison Walls Could Talk, would they reprimand correctional officers for the disrespectful ways that they treat inmates?

Would they express their disapproval of how they pay slave wages to work?

Would they order institutions to shut down the cramped up twelve man holes that they call cells?

Would they condone the poor medical treatment we receive?

If These Prison Walls Could Talk, would they ask for the resignations of those officers who come to work intoxicated and take their personal problems out on the inmates?

Would they employ more counselors to help get prisoners better programs?

If These Prison Walls Could Talk, would they try to give the youth better guidance, and try to prevent them from ending up as a member of a gang?

Would they tell the story of so many who lost their lives, alone, on the inside?

Would they console those who lost a family member and was unable to attend the funeral?

If These Prison Walls Could Talk, what would they really say?

I would like to know…..

Hard Body Snatch

Westbury, Newcastle, N.Y.

Chapter Eight
Change

H-Block is our last unit. This is where most of the inmates are preparing themselves for reentry, back into society. Statistically, the numbers say that three out of every four felons will return to prison within two years after their release.

- According to the American Corrections Association, the average daily cost per state prison inmate per day in the U.S. is $67.55. State prisons held 253,300 inmates for drug offences in 2005. That means that states spent approximately $17,110,415 per day to imprison drug offenders, or $6,245,301,475 per year.

- States spent $42.89 billion on corrections in 2005 alone. To compare, states only pent $24.69 billion on public assistance. From 1984 to 1996, California built 21 new prisons and only one new university.

- Between 1979 and 2000, the number of additional prisons ranged from 19 prisons in Missouri to 120 prisons in Texas. The growth in Texas equates to an extraordinary average annual increase of 5.7 additional prisons per year, over a 221 year period. Over this time frame, Texas has increased its prisons by a stunning 706 percent.
  –A Nation Incarcerated: The American Goal Crisis.

While comprehending what has taken place with the United States penal system, those who are enmeshed in certain injustices must understand that a change must take place. Not only in the courts or with Congress but within ones' own self. Without first changing your thought process, you will never be able to change your actions. Without changing your actions, your conditions will continue to remain the same; or perhaps even get worse. In many instances, you as an individual stand apart from all others of your kind, and are today exactly what you have made of yourself. Not only by your thoughts, but by your actions. For those of you who search fervently for the answer on how to escape the drudgery of your past, I beseech you to cultivate your mind. With the implementation of cultivating your thoughts, there arises a new sun on the horizon. Old concepts pass away, while new ways of thinking give birth to strength and direction.

Understand that change is a process. Each of us grows at a different rate. Our degrees of development often times take decades or even a lifetime. For millions of years, while the sun set in the west, it left man in the darkness. Then after a period of time, he discovered oil, which in turn helped to give him light. These changes were the result of his thinking.

Pain and suffering is also a means to change. When an individual becomes conscious, he is able to ascertain all lessons of past struggles. Whether it be mental, physical or emotional. I ask that you open your mind as I give you an illustration on why experiencing certain hardships can be a gateway to the necessary changes that are needed in order for criminality to be renounced by an adherence to the law.

The Butterfly

One day, two brothers were walking along, in the park when they came across a butterfly in the last stages of emerging from its cocoon.

"Look at that!" The younger brother exclaimed in amazement.

"What?" The older sibling replied, while looking in the other direction.

"It's a butterfly! It needs help!"

"Wai-"

Before the older brother had a chance to stop his younger brother, he ran over to the tree, plucked the cocoon from its branch and carefully opened it up. After grabbing the butterfly by its wings, he tossed it up into the air, expecting it to fly. Instead, it floundered to the ground. Repeating the same act, he continued to get the same results. For some strange reason, the butterfly wouldn't take flight. Unable to figure out what was wrong, the younger brother turned to his older brother, with questioning eyes, "what's wrong with it?!" He asked, sympathetically.

Pleased that the opportunity to teach his younger brother a valuable life lesson had presented itself, the older brother began to explain, "The cocoon is part of a strengthening process for the butterfly. While inside, it metamorphoses from a caterpillar. It changes from one of the ugliest creatures on earth to perhaps the most beautiful insect that has ever been created. During the time of its imprisonment, it grows wings. Those wings must be strong enough in order for it to fly."

"What do you mean?"

Choosing his words carefully, the older brother answered, "The butterfly must be allowed to break free from the cocoon on its own. Any interference from the outside will hinder its progress. It is one of many phases that it must go through in order for it to be able to adapt to the necessary changes. —So it is with life. As you get older, you will begin to understand that all of the struggles you face will be for the betterment of who you were created to be. There's no one on earth who doesn't face trials and tribulations, but most important is who you become after you've risen above your challenges."

America is the land of the second chance. When the prison gates open, the path ahead should be directed towards a better life.

-THE O.G. WISE MAN

If These Prison Walls Could Talk

If These Prison Walls Could Talk, they would discuss at length, the many struggles that men face each day.

They would tell the story of those who walked inside of the institutions with no education, learned law, and in the end became legal assistants.

They would talk about all of the so called King Pins, murderers and thugs, who cry after receiving heart felt letters from a family member.

If These Prison Walls Could Talk, they would remind the inhabitants to stay mindful of past mistakes, their present situations and to never take the future for granted.

They would urge the young men to change their ways.

They would apprise the illegal immigrants of their rights and call for fair wages inside of all Unicor Factories.

If These Prison Walls Could Talk, they would say many things that the government wouldn't want to hear.

If these Prison Walls Could Talk, society would become more caring.

La Ron "Bink" Pashal

Rhode Island

Did you know that seventy percent of prisoners in the U.S. are non-white, even though non-whites make up only about a third of the population of this country? One out of every twenty black males over the age of 18 are in prison. That compares to one in one hundred and eighty white males over the age of 18. In five states, between one and thirteen and one in fourteen black men are in prison. One in nine African American males will spend at least one year in jail over the course of their lifetimes.

Did you also know that most drug offenders are white? Five times as many whites use drugs as blacks, yet blacks comprise the great majority of drug offenders who are sent to prison. Of the 253,300 state prison inmates serving time for drug offenses at year end of 2005, 113,500 (44.8%) were black; 51,100 (20.2%) were Hispanic; 72,300 (28.5%) were white. The non-violent prison population alone is larger than the combined populations of Wyoming and Alaska.

A Nation Incarcerated: The American Goal Crisis

Strolling into the Supervisor of Educations Office on 11-9-10, with my folder in my hand, I sat down opposite of the short, Hispanic man, who was engaged in a conversation on the phone. I really didn't have too much time to waste. Although I was in prison, I was a very busy man. My schedule was just as tight as a CEO's of a big corporation. I woke up at 4:30 a.m., worked out, ate a light breakfast, went to work, on my lunch break, I conducted interviews, studied psychology, did research for one of my books or squeezed in a letter or two. That was only the first half of my day. After 4:00 p.m. count, I was back in the gym, training a couple of individuals. From there, I either taught the "Back To The Future" class, studied real estate, designed clothes, worked on one of my books, studied the stock market or gave my attention to one of the much needed problems that may have been brewing on the unit. At times I was so busy that people had to make appointments to come up to my cell to talk to me. I didn't have any time to waste and, I wasn't trying to be involved in anything that was counter- productive.

After finishing up his phone call, the Supervisor of Education hung up the receiver and turned his attention to me. I was only there to pick up my Instructors Certificate for the **"We Got Next"** urban literature class that I had just taught, and really didn't have time for small talk. "I received a lot of good reviews about your class, Mr. Dolphin." He stated with a smile on his face.

"Is that right?" I smiled back.

"Yes sir. Many of the guys have been requesting that we run the class for another ten weeks. Can you handle that?"

Having already been aware of how many people wanted me to continue to do another class, I responded, "If they want to learn, then I'm going to do my best to teach them."

Studying me for a moment, he inquired, "Mr. Dolphin, are you in some type of gang?"

"Gang?!" I laughed, caught off guard by such a foolish question. "What made you ask me something like that?"

"Cause, I see how much these guys around here respect you. Being the type of institution this is, I was just curious, that's all."

"Is that right."

"Yea. I'm aware that over eighty percent of this compound is affiliated with some sort of gang, click, car, crew or whatever you want to call it. If you're not in a gang, then how do you avoid confrontations?"

I laughed again.

"Why are you laughing?" He questioned.

It was my turn now. "You want me to be straight up with you?" I turned serious."There is no confrontations." I replied, while looking him square in the eye. "Although I'm not the same person that I once was when I first entered this place, several years ago, those who are really from the streets recognize a real man when they see one. I carry myself in a respectable manner. Therefore, I am given the due respect that my hand calls for. On every level, I am no-nonsense. Understanding the way that this environment works, I give everyone that I come in contact with respect. In doing so, I demand that same respect in return."

"So, you're actually saying that although you have changed, the individuals on the compound can still sense who you once were?"

"Basically. Although I am refined and have a smooth interior, my exterior often shows traces of my rough past. In a way, I feel that it is bad, but on the other hand, I feel that it helps me when it comes to being able to get through to some one that you may not be able to. It also helps me in my teaching."

"In what way?"

I paused for a second, then answered, "By coming from the other side of the fence, I am better equipped to be able to relate to whatever goes on around here. Without a bias eye. Although I don't always get the response that I may be looking for, I feel that I have helped solve more problems in this place than the staff has."

By the time I had left the Supervisor Of Educations office that morning, I was quite sure that he had a better understanding of who I was, what I stood for and exactly what I was trying to accomplish through out the institution.

At the time of this writing, there were 218 federal prisons, 38,000 staff members and 217,000 prisoners. (According to Federal Bureau of Prisons)

- 1.6 million people in state and federal prisons.
- Over 700,000 people in local jails.

A Call To Action

Joseph Nicks

Washington D.C.

My name is Joseph Nicks. I am 46 years old at the time of this writing. I have been locked up for the past 30 years in federal prison.

I once read that first impressions don't count nearly as much as an overall performance. I have learned from being confined at such an early age in my life that such things as being smart didn't mean the same as being wise; being tough was not the same as being strong; and being shown was not the same as being lead.

Reflection

I think back about my past, and all of the things that lead me to my present state in life. As I became more conscious, I began to feel remorse, sorrow and even shame. But as I've learned to pray over the years, God has kept me holding on. Allowing me to maintain my sanity. I watched with a heavy heart as so many young men came into the system, just as I had done. Many of them were uneducated and without a mother or a father in their lives to give them the proper guidance that they needed. Some of these young men are never going home. They wake up each morning finding themselves trapped in prison for the rest of their lives.

One of my biggest fears while being incarcerated was losing my family ties; not knowing if I would ever see my loved ones again.

As time ticked away, I got stronger. I began to understand why I was here and what role I was created to play. From that day on, my aspirations has been to help the younger men that would come into the prison system; in which I now reside. I know that I have been blessed after all of these years, and I thank The Creator for making all blessings possible.

If I could start my life over again, I would not change what happened along the way. Although a lot of things that I was doing was generally wrong, being under age at the time, I would not have the opportunity to express my growth and maturity.

I realize as I begin to use my understanding in depth that nobody is perfect and that we as human beings are subject to make disastrous mistakes in life…This is how we learn…. If we allow ourselves to. I now see myself as a productive product that can provide values to society, as well as, benefits that are social, symbolic and psychological….

My main objective through out my life as I view it now, is to stay focused and ask questions whenever I'm making a decision.

Vision

As I see the youth today, I think back to when I was a young man; and I refused to listen to my mother and father. I can only feel sympathetic for them. Just the thought of how hurt they must have been still brings tears to my eyes.

Today, I understand that young people need a lot of attention, love and answers. Principles, values, love, respect, loyalty and understanding are very important. There are churches, mosques, recreational facilities, counseling fieldtrips, etc. that can be used as outlets for learning and shaping character.

As hard as it may be at times, we must lead our young people by the hand; instruct them on what must be done in order for them to be successful in life, and show them how to make their communities better…. If they are not getting the fatherly love…Hard hand, which most of them seek, then we as men/women must give it to them…. It is our responsibility, if we expect them to conduct themselves in a proper manner. We must place mentors in position to guide them and help them become the doctors, lawyers, policemen, politicians, judges, statesmen and business owners of tomorrow. If we do these things, I am willing to guarantee that the percentage rate of youth who are involved in crime will decrease.

The way that you strengthen and regenerate the community now is by providing a lot of counseling opportunities for our young. Counseling provided by people with first-hand knowledge and experience can and will be beneficial to the understanding of the young.

When you talk about reducing youth involvement with guns, drugs and gangs, you must first check out their family and neighborhood associations. What kind of environment are they living in…. The conditions of the schools, churches and mosques… Are there any recreational facilities close by.

WE CAN hold seminars on what guns can do to people. How drugs alter your thinking process and how gangs pressure the youth into doing the wrong things; like hooking school, fighting or using drugs and alcohol.

WE MUST take pride in educating our youth... More than anything, they need someone to talk to, who will listen to what they have to say. Who will not be so judgmental. Someone who will help usher them along the way...

WE MUST break the cycle... I ask that all of you who are willing to join forces with Cook City Publications, Breaking The Chainz, and Headed Nowhere Fast make a pledge to help clean up our communities, educate the youth, decrease the sweltering prison population and stand on social and economic equality...

If These Prison Walls Could Talk what would they tell the youth?

The Merriam Webster Dictionary Terms

- Freedom – The quality or state of being free; Independence.
- Justice – The administration of what is just (as by assigning merited rewards or punishment). The administration of law, fairness; Righteousness.
- Equality – Of the same measure, quantity, value, quality, number, degree, or status as another. (Opportunity). Impartial; free from extremes.

Each year prisoners represent an economic value to the home community, and has been placed elsewhere. As an economic being the person would spend money at or near his/her area of residence; typically an inner city. Imprisonment displaces that economic activity. Instead of buying a snack in a local deli, the prisoner makes a purchase inside the prison commissary. The removal may represent a loss of economic value to the home community, but it is a boom to the prison community. Each prisoner represents as much as $25,000 in income in which the community is located; not to mention the value of constructing the prison facility in the first place. This can be a massive transfer of value. A young male worth a few thousand dollars of support to children and local purchases is transformed into a $25,000 financial asset to a rural community. The economy of the rural community is artificially amplified, and the local city economy is artificially deflated….

- This according to Race, Prison, Poverty History is a weapon.com

Before leaving H-Black, join me in my final interview:

November 14, 2010

Dr, Kevin E. Dolphin: Thank you for allowing me a few minutes of your time.

Inmate: If you're doin' somethin', I know it has some substance to it, so you can always call on me, anytime.

Dr. Kevin E. Dolphin: Thank you. For our readers, could you state your name?

Inmate: Crudup Depaul. My homeboys call me Pace.

Dr. Kevin E. Dolphin: Is it cool if I call you Pace?

Inmate: No doubt.

Dr. Kevin E. Dolphin: Okay, Pace. Where are you from?

Inmate: I'm from Newhaven, Connecticut.

Dr. Kevin E. Dolphin: How long have you been locked up?

Inmate: I been in prison for almost six years.

Dr. Kevin E. Dolphin: Is your mother still alive?

Inmate: Yes.

Dr. Kevin E. Dolphin: If there was one thing that you could say to her at this very moment, what would it be?

Inmate: I would tell her that I love her with all of my heart and that I'm sorry for all of my defaults.

Dr. Kevin E. Dolphin: Who was your biggest influence when you were growing up?

Inmate: My mother.

Dr. Kevin E. Dolphin: Why?

Inmate: Me and her had this talk a couple of weeks ago, and she told me that she felt that she hadn't done enough. When she said that, I laughed. Man, she spoiled me! She did more than enough! That includes love, guidance, material things, and everything else. She was the perfect example when it came to someone to look up to.

Dr. Kevin E. Dolphin: What is one important thing that you have learned since you've been locked up?

Inmate: Humility.

Dr. Kevin E. Dolphin: If you could do one thing over in life, what would it be?

Inmate: I really don't have any regrets. But, I would like to spend more time with my mother and tell her that I love her a trillion times! He laughs.

Dr. Kevin E. Dolphin: That's love! How do you feel about education?

Inmate: It's a must! You can never stop learning. Without educating yourself, you will never be able to advance in life. It's sad when I see people stuck in the projects, content wit' their situations and never searching for a better!

Dr. Kevin E. Dolphin: What part did education play in your life?

Inmate: I had a chance to further my education, but I chose the streets instead. Knowing what I know now, I would have stayed in school. Education is the foundation of change. When you don't know nothin', how can you change?! What can you change?! That's deep, ain't it?

Dr. Kevin E. Dolphin: It sure is. Thank you for your assistance, Pace.

Inmate: You got it.

If These Prison Walls Could Talk

If These Prison Walls Could Talk, would they laugh at the ignorance of those who refuse to change and continue to destroy their communities with drugs and violence?

Would they get mad, close all of the cell doors and refuse to let those who are shut in back out into society?

Would they judge each prisoner as a whole, instead of as an individual?

Would they support the so called WAR ON DRUGS, or would they rally for treatment, speak out about the Smart Sentencing Act, hold law makers accountable for criminal justice reform and help reduce the recidivism rate?

If These Prison Walls Could Talk, would they change the way that our nation views the penal system?

Would they begin the correct all of the wrongs that take place, deep within its bowels each day?

Would they dispel the myth of rehabilitation and call punishment exactly what it is, or would they reestablish the system and invoke social equality?

If These Prison Walls Could Talk, what would they really say?

The O.G. Wise Man

Redemption

Co-founder of the notorious Crips gang, Stanley 'Tookie' Williams spent decades on death row before being executed on December 13, 2005. After years of reflecting on his life of turmoil, the former O.G. tried his best to correct the mistakes of his troubled past. He wrote several award-winning omit-gang childrens books and was also a candidate for the Nobel Peace Prize. Despite his valiant efforts at Redemption, his plea for clemency was denied by then, California Governor, Arnold Schwarzenegger.

In the wake of 'Tookies' execution, activist, entertainers, athletes and human rights leaders rallied against what many felt to be a grave injustice. Legendary rapper KRS-One spoke out vehemently on the situation. "I couldn't help asking myself over and over again, did 'Tooke' have to die? Did Stan 'Tookie' Williams really have to die? Son, husband, father of two, grandfather of three, minister, changed man, was there no way to pay that debt back to society other than the execution of a transformed man, who held on to his claim of innocence all of the way to the end? "Tookie' had to die? I don't think so.

As a reckless and misguided youth, who's mind was often polluted with drugs, Stanley 'Tookie' Williams was unaware of the enormous power and influence that he possessed as a leader. Using his prowess in the wrong manner, he helped to create an unthinkable monster, where thousands of young Crips, Bloods, Disciples and gang members, all of different shades of hues aimlessly shoot, maim and torment one another, on a daily basis. Coming to terms with what many others looked upon as unforgivable, he took personal responsibility for what he deemed as acts of ignorance. Was it enough? Not for the anarchy of unforgiving delegates who sit at the top of our court system. Redemption was a word that didn't exist in their law books.

Owning the wrongs that he had committed, but unwilling to compromise his integrity for something that he insisted he hadn't done, 'Tookie' maintained his innocence until that final hour. –He spoke, "Teach the youth how to avoid our destructive footsteps. Teach them to strive for a higher education. Teach them to promote peace. And teach them to focus on rebuilding the neighborhoods that you, I and others like us so blindly helped to destroy."

In conclusion, I ask, is there a such a thing as Redemption? You decide.

The United States Judicial System is in dire need of change. The only way that those changes can be made is by support and demands by tax payers and voters. Congress will do nothing, if allowed to side step and negate the facts. Although some responsibility must be given to those who commit crime, some of that weight falls on the governments shoulders.

It makes no sense to treat drug offenders or illegal immigrants, who have not committed violent crimes the same way that other violent prisoners are treated. For those who are in need, intensive drug treatment should be administered; While those who enter this country illegally should be placed in separate camps, tried fairly, then sent back to their countries.

Creative solutions to our overcrowded prison system should be lobbied for, instead of stiffer laws and harsher punishment. Without some sort of education, the criminal minded will remain just that. In order for a person to consider change he/she must be presented with the opportunity. Trying to force a certain way of thinking or lifestyle on an individual may work for a short period of time, but in the long run, it will never pan out. From experience, I can tell you that trying to force someone to do something before they are ready will only cause contention.

Injustice and inequality must be replaced with adherence to the constitution, just as unlawfulness and immorality must be given up for ethical principles. Nothing will ever be given to a people of any color if at first they don't show that they deserve what they are fighting for. The numbers and statistics in this book don't lie. History repeats itself.

For those of you who claim that you are tired of being treated unfairly, I urge you to do something about it. Without first standing for something, you will continue to fall for anything. If you continue to play the same game that so many before you have played, then it is inevitable for you to get exactly what they got.

It is a fact that many of the laws imposed by the courts are unjust, but what is to be said about the millions of young men who stand out on the street corners selling drugs, killing one another and committing all sorts of other felonious crimes? Should your uncaring acts go un-penalized or should you be brought before a righteous panel of your peers, sanctioned and helped to see that if you are unwilling to change your corrupt way of thinking, you are a detriment to your community, a danger to yourself and others, a liability to your family and therefore will be deemed unfit for society.

If These Prison Walls Could Talk, they would tell you to educate the next generation, because without your help, your sons and daughters will occupy the same bed space that you once did. The chainz will remain, the doors of recidivism will continue to revolve and the population of the United States penal system will continue to grow without CRIMINAL JUSTICE REFORM.

I give thanks to all of the men who helped me put together this very much needed piece of literary work. May each of your families look beyond your faults and be ever so proud of you.

Quotes and References

Quotes and References

References

Charles Lemos 2010.

Stephen Fry.

U.S. Bureau of Justice .

American Correction Association.

Ericksons' 8 Stages of Psychological Development.

Tom Bowman.

Patriot News.

Dr. Martin Luther King Jr.

Malcom X.

Julian Rotters Locus Of Control.

Marcus M. Garvey. (Message To The People).

WEB Dubois.

The Souls Of Black Folk.

Alfred Adler.

The Bible.

The Holy Quran

Epictetus

Ellen Harper

Carl Rogers

ASCA/PEW.

Newt Gingrich.

Tom Roy.

Minnesota Commission of Corrections.

Albert Bandura.

B.F. Skinner.

Waters & Gusec.

Widom.

Wikipedia.

Federal Bureau of Prisons.

Race, Prison, Poverty Is A Weapon.